The Monterians

The Monterians

Charles Hurst

ISBN: 9798595993203 (paperback)

CHAPTER 1

May

Jack Strickland stood looking east into The Bay, the morning air still and warmed from the nightly chill that accommodated the sun's retreat. The fog lifted slowly as if in preparation for the many tourists who would soon leisurely amble back and forth down the popular shoreline path, which paralleled Ocean View Blvd. It was late May and the light was out early, breaking its rays through the mist and over the water in unhurried painting of shimmering blue over its canvass, dotted by whitecaps that broke lazily toward the sand's flattened edge. The Bay had many tones. It sported days, like the present, when in fine temperament or could cast a frigid, cloudy gray over sky and sea if slightly moody. If downright irritable, a cold mist might throw itself and blanket the town, which it did many mornings of the winter months and felt righteous in the act as snow was deprived of the region.

Even though only 7:00 a.m., Jack could sense that The Bay would exhibit its finest display for the thousands of people who would roam around it until evening. The tourists filled the city between the months of May and September. They would be out soon, pouring coffee in their stomachs and placing ice packs on their headaches from too many rum flavored mixers, wine and domestic hops from the night before. By 9:00 a.m., the natives would patiently walk, jog and bike around the numerous gawking visitors who clumsily made their way from Fisherman's Wharf to Cannery Row to Lover's Point, back to The Wharf and finally returned to their bed and breakfasts, where spirit-filled dreams lapped waves against their pillows.

Monterey contained three types who could be observed at the many cafes, bars, bistros and shops. The first was the vacationer, easily spotted by the hanging camera and long gaze at what was surely a first glimpse of Eden. They were transient and spent obscene amounts of money in stride with the locals while they captured the Garden in hurried slices with their digitals; pieces of fruit that would frame their bedrooms and desks as a constant reminder that they were eventually cast out and returned to the appropriate classes. The second type consisted of those who worked in the city but were unable to afford to live there. They labored mostly in the service industry, tolerated by day as long as they were safely locked up at night in the dirtier beachside closet down the road known as Seaside. The enormous cost of living in the city of Monterey insured the working classes were to remain exactly that while in its district, and while on leisure, they did it elsewhere.

The highest caste was the native Monterian. The residing Monterian was almost as easily spotted as the transient tourist. The Monterian jogged gaily down the shoreline but did not revel in it. The Monterian dressed fashionably casual as if by accident all of the proper name brands mysteriously fell into place on the way to coffee at Cannery Row or "The Row" as they quaintly spoke of the old cannery buildings, now transformed into exhibits and expensive shops, which sat in view of the ghost launching pads from The Wharf. The Wharf, which in a previous era brought boatloads of sardines to be painstakingly processed and packaged, many times into the midnight hour. The Monterians were hideously clean cut in attire and manner while guising under the pretense that they weren't. Most were extremely wealthy.

It was only a subject of irony that Monterey had not begun as a place of such grandeur. Only after the last world war, the immense wealth was hoarded by a select few who had the foresight to monopolize The Bay's resource. Cannery Row had been named, not for its attraction, but its industry in the 1940s. The morning bells and whistles of varied tones, which signified different companies, called hundreds of poor workers from their huts and shacks on the hills to begin what would often be twelve and fifteen-hour days in the noxious stench of the sardine lines. For the influential this climate continued, noted by Steinbeck and Ricketts, the silvery water largely belonged to the cannery owners. Then in 1964 as The Bay surrendered its sacrifice completely, the industry suddenly ceased, the corporations departed, and the natives who remained, planted the seeds unknowingly that would be nourished by the poor community to sprout into generations of tourist wealth. And these descendents of new prosperity would remain so, neither realizing nor caring that if the sardine bridges, which still crossed The Row today, functioned in their proper cause, they would more likely than not, toil in them as their forefathers.

Jack Strickland, although he contained a deep adoration for Monterey Bay, was not a native himself. That is to say he was not born there. Strickland was born in Illinois and first arrived in the bay area at eighteen years old, freshly graduated from high school and via the United States Navy. The navy instantly recognized Strickland's smarts at the testing board and placed him in Intelligence, which required a year in the Russian Proficiency Course located at the Defense Language Institute or "The Hill" as the locals curtly referred to it.

Monterey did not hold affection for the military. In fact, it could be contrived by many witnesses on The Hill that it held nothing but disdain. Highly liberal with higher Ivy League educations, furnished by the sweat of their ancestors, Monterians could be said to have a belief in the military in only a vague concept, providing the concept was not concrete in their backyard. Over the years many proposals were put forth by the city council to the White House that perhaps the Defense Language Institute, fine scholastic reputation it had, would be more suited in a different vicinity—say Fort Hood, Texas, where the locals had more than the abstract belief in the uniform. Transplanted to a place where the returning sorority coeds for the summer would not be forced to observe the crew cut and tattoo. The natives' proposals always fell on deaf ears and thus gave the locals only an uneasy truce that the soldiers, as the days of old line workers, were at least kept out of sight on top of The Hill. Most of the time.

Jack Strickland, now seventeen years senior to his first arrival, remembered well. He had been brought up poor and did not conceal this fact by entering the city as an enlisted seaman. His first expedition down The Hill from Franklin Street to Del Monte, Jack had actually worn his issued uniform and thought the insignia would be a welcome sight as it would have certainly been in his hometown among its own small coffee shops and bars. In Monterey, it was not. Jack recalled that it wasn't as much as what the natives specifically said about the matter but what they did not. And they spent a great deal of time not saying a lot, instructing young Jack that the worst insults can sometimes be received with the least volume. The unsuspecting youth had gone downtown to a pub once, this time leaving the uniform in the barracks. In the bar, he politely asked a girl of his approximate age to dance. He had mistakenly thought some impression was to come forth from his study of Russian. The result was a failure as her trained social context promptly declined but only after a long quizzical look, which stated perplexity at being addressed to begin with. Not assisting matters was another young man who obviously did not live up The Hill. He overheard the encounter and raised his beer glass in mock salute, which caused Jack's ears to burn even more than the girl and her friends' low murmurs. He left the pub exactly as he entered it a few minutes afterward.

"Sheeit . . . you hit on a native?" his roommate had jested when Jack sported the incident in the more familiar Enlisted Club just past the gate.

"I didn't *hit* on her. I asked her to dance," he replied, still feeling the heat in his temples.

"Asked? Partner, let me tell you something or two. You don't ask them nothin'. I've been here six months, and I don't ask them nothin' either."

"Why?"

"*Why*, he says. Boy, you don't get it. Look around you. See that bay? That bay's made of bucks and so is everyone who lives here . . . except us. *They* don't like us. *They* don't like anybody who ain't got moola. And I mean a *lot* of it. But especially us. You know what one of those houses cost here in the city?"

"No," Jack answered, feeling more ignorant as the conversation progressed.

"About a million. No shit. One *million* dollars. And that's the house that girl went back to tonight after you pissed her off. Some enlisted guy who shares a room with one or two other guys. They hardly talk to the officers let alone us. Dance . . . . My ass, man."

So Jack never tried to speak or dance with another local again. In fact, for the rest of his stay there, Jack stuck to the E-Club instead of the local taverns. But there was one place that spoke to him without animosity. The shoreline path, which ran from Fisherman's Wharf to The Row and headed to 17 Mile Drive, which transported one to the rising cliffs of Big Sur. Especially at night it spoke . . . when the natives had retired to their small mansions or the bars downtown. The waves spoke softly, reminding Jack that although wealthy, they had witnessed when they were not always so. He spent hours walking up and down the vacant path along the water, climbing out to formations at low tide, feet away from where the foam crashed into the corral ridden rocks.

"Monterey Bay doesn't care if I'm on The Hill, does it?" he asked no one on a particular night, halfway through his study and two roommates later. The ocean answered methodically with no heed to rank or title as it did a hundred and a thousand years ago.

He completed the Russian Basic Course and left The Hill a year after and swore privately that one day he would be good enough for that dance. Jack finished his enlistment three years later and found that even while on leave in Singapore, Naval Intelligence wasn't as illustrious as the recruiter had portrayed it when Jack had signed on.

But he didn't return to Monterey . . . not immediately.

When he finished his time with the navy, Jack returned to Illinois and took advantage of the G.I. Bill. He studied pre-engineering, finding the necessity to teach himself algebra to complete chemistry and trigonometry to survive physics.

But Jack endured. He found one vouch for service in the military was the basic discipline it gave him to show up for 8:00 a.m. classes and complete assignments to the best of his ability when others did not. His pre-engineering became real engineering, in which Strickland settled on the electrical genre. He graduated in the upper portion of his class at the age of twenty-six.

However, this accomplishment was not the crowning point of the Strickland saga. It was true that his parents and small town he was raised in could not have been prouder, and even Jack himself could not have wished for greater satisfaction. His starting salary was sixty thousand dollars a year—over four times as much as he earned in the navy when he left, noted daily from the discharge pin he kept on his desk to remind him of his true beginning. His ascension up the summit occurred when he realized a subtle dissatisfaction in doing a job for sixty thousand dollars a year for someone else. So he and a friend in the company, Everett, began the great *what if* that all successful entrepreneurs can sentimentally gaze back upon, years after the actual success. Jack and Everett fancied themselves hobbyist inventors in the many evenings and late nights of Jack's basement, which was filled with small contraptions and sheet designs.

And one day it was no longer just a fancy.

Everett, after his own graduation, had studied further and developed a forte in telecommunication and radio wave propagation. The idea began amusingly to the annoyance of dropped cell phone calls that often aggravated the masses.

Engineers, by nature, cannot help themselves once a problem presents itself for solvability. Everett and Jack were no exceptions. Their exploit began much like one who attempts to unravel the Rubik's cube for the sheer sake of doing so.

The great *what if*.

A new, smaller size chip that could fit in a compact cell phone, which contained slightly altered transmission to the cell towers, insuring a better delivery from the caller. Although nothing which would revolutionize an industry, the Micro Amp Transit, or MAT, as they named it, would serve for better quality service in an extremely competitive industry.

After three years of tests and retests on the device for long term durability, the two engineers patented their invention. Jack and Everett bargained themselves lucky if the novelty brought in a little extra cash flow and possibly a bit of recognition early in their careers. Something to market themselves for other peoples' companies. A few small outfits might show interest in the device. They might even get published in a collegial magazine.

However, much to the stunned disbelief of the two inventors, it sold to a major telecommunications corporation a few months after the patent was sealed. And several magazines with great zeal did note the fact and gave widespread interest to other competitors as well. Jack and Everett had made their first million within the close of the year. That was five years ago. Jack, now thirty-five, had a net worth of six point two million dollars, one point seven of the sum included in his five bedroom house, which sat within view of the shoreline path and Monterey's aqua mirror that reflected it.

Jack gazed at his beloved bay with long-time nostalgia. The tide drifted back into the sea at the cove, the same inlet where he went out at low tide years ago and sat on the rocks at night while his military comrades either studied or drank at the E-Club. It was Saturday and he deemed it best to let other people take care of business on Saturdays. Several cafes would be open soon. He thought he should get a paper and have breakfast on his second morning as an authentic local.

And the waves still acknowledged him with the identical indifference they did seventeen years ago as he began to walk down to the shoreline path.

◆ ◆ ◆

The summer's glistening blue, as Jack predicted, remained throughout the day. The tourists ambled to and fro in short sleeve shirts and ball caps of various sorts as if in defiance of their every day positions of which they would shortly return. The sun began to set in the west, arcing past Pebble Beach and over Big Sur, where it would disappear only to reignite at dawn across the foothills that gently dropped into soft landing on the sands of Monterey.

Jack had changed clothes. Natives knew from long habit, which tourists did not, when the sun went down it was prudent to change from Monterey day clothes, which would suffice as the rays warmed The Bay, to night attire when the descent would follow with evening chill. They also realized the necessity of carrying a jacket at all times as there was no specific contract, even with the mid-summer months, to remain temperate throughout the entire day shift. It was quite common in all sea towns for an unexpected and unwelcome fog to suddenly intrude the region unannounced and remain for indeterminate durations, dropping the temperature many degrees in the process.

Fisherman's Wharf, although busy and congested during the day, with the exception of the occasional guttural bark of the slumbering sea lions, would become ghostly silent at night. The tourists drifted with the coming dusk, out of the restaurants and shops, arms bundling purchased ocean shells and shirts and cups and postcards. The chill sent them on temporary reprieve to regroup in the many pubs downtown or The Row, where they ventured protected from the sea breeze by the buildings, which lined parallel to it. Structures that once stood witness to John Steinbeck himself discussing new novelties of The Bay over steamed beer with his cherished friend and ocean-adventuring colleague, the mentioned Edward "Doc" Ricketts.

Jack walked from the intersection of Fifth and Ocean View Boulevard, the location of his youthful cove, to The Row. He noticed the sparse remaining cars on the street along the wooden fence that ran next to the path where he had once parked his second-hand motorcycle, bought from a departing student from The Hill. He could have parked downtown or at one of the many paid lots as money was not the factor it was years ago but chose the fifteen minute walk for reasons of simple reminiscence.

He dropped down to The Aquarium—home to exotic fishes, sea plants and sharks from all over the world. And people came from all over the world to stand in the long morning lines to gain entrance in the summer. Turning right, he patiently maneuvered through clusters of tourists and curved into a coffee shop he discovered the previous day. He gave the owner a familiar wave, entitled to Jack as he now deemed himself a true local of the city. Jack felt no rush as it was early in the evening, and he had no wide selection of friends who would be waiting on his arrival. He had been a resident of The Bay for officially two full days—unless he counted the time on The Hill, and according to the natives, they did not. Yesterday he furnished his house from the moving truck, which had arrived earlier than scheduled. This had irritated him as he had only landed in the very small morning hours himself after a long three-day drive from Illinois. Jack immediately noticed that his modest furniture was not the smartest match for the Monterey domain. And he didn't have enough furnishings to fill the newly acquired space. His bachelor status left three of the five rooms bare and only one fully stocked. He decided to go out this week on a shopping spree to the local outlets to remedy the situation. He could equip one room with a pool table and a bar. Create a guest space and deck out the living area to the true genre of a gentleman spinster. Maybe even hire an interior decorator as he didn't exactly rely on his male instinct in such matters. Why not? He was secure after five years that the money was to last.

And, of course, the spare rooms could be recreated again into children's centers. However, at thirty-five, Jack was not completely beaming with confidence. He was not "playing the field" as the saying goes, even though the playing ground was now greatly tilted to his side since his newly acclaimed wealth. Even prior to his grand innovation, he found his status as a newly graduated engineer elevated him several rungs on the social hierarchy from his days of sloshing around on an aircraft carrier. He was not dazzling in looks but not unattractive either, with slightly thinning hair only in custom with his age and a runner's physique, conditioned from his early days of basic training. The only military habit he still kept five times a week. But during his elevation up Darwin's ladder, he found that a man's appeal to the other half was directly proportional to his income. And it was apparent that this allure had become greatly magnified the very month it was known that his invention took hold as the young female tellers at the bank seemed to instantly realize his charm and wit, which had gone greatly unnoticed beforehand. This realization made Jack two parts thankful and three parts cynical. He was unaware that the rumors of his bachelorhood were already in circulation in Monterey's fairer society. The local paper had given a snippet of his upcoming arrival after he finalized the purchase of the house a month ago.

But Jack still felt himself as an oddity, somebody that everyone began to recognize, but no one knew. Already to a few natives, he was the inventor of the MAT. That much was realized before they had even set eyes upon his hairline or person. And although transplanted from the Midwest, this fact gave him the proper waiver for Monterey's custom path to citizenship and promptly opened the velvet rope ahead of everyone else.

Jack stepped into "Bully's" after the coffee shop. Bully's was a restaurant and lounge bar, which he remembered seventeen years ago under a different name that he could not recollect. He had stopped by during his house purchase trip weeks ago and talked briefly with someone who said he periodically endorsed the tavern. Since Jack was new and alone in the city, he reasoned that nothing would be lost by taking his chances, better here as anywhere else. He walked through the thick oak door and noted the man-sized statue of a surly sea captain holding his pipe, mocking those who entered. Jack glanced around nervously at the couples and groups already in the lounge area until his eye caught the person at the end of the bar who spoke noisily to the bartender. The man stopped in mid-sentence upon seeing Jack and with a remembered wave, motioned him over. He drank a burgundy, purplish type of concoction with an orange slice and a long straw. It was obvious from his amplified tone that it was not the first.

"Jack!" he hailed for himself as well as most of the lounge. "Are you finally arrived, old boy?"

Jack raised his own arm and felt curious eyes upon him as he went over and took the seat next to the man.

"I'm sorry. I'm pretty good with names, but it usually takes me twice."

"Sure," the man replied, waving him down. "Lots of new people at once. Name's Bledsloe. Anthony Bledsloe by tradition, but I go by Tony out of it."

"Tony it is," Jack said, shaking his hand. "And actually, you're the only one in town who I've met. Except for the realtor a month ago." Tony boomed the laughter of all large, post-athletic men who have failed to recall they are no longer in attendance of an after school pep rally. The lounge again looked briefly away from their drinks and conversations to the bar. Jack immediately gathered this man was not only accustomed to mass attention but gregariously reveled in it.

"You bought the place on the bayside a few weeks ago," Tony stated.

"Is there an underground network?" Jack replied humorously. "But yeah, about a month ago I got it. Like I told you last time, when I flew in for the close. Just officially moved the furniture in yesterday."

"Network in The Bay? Old boy, you'd better believe it . . . hey, hold that thought. Sarge!" he called across to the other end of the bar and brought a tall man over who wore a crew cut. "What are you drinking tonight, Jacko?"

"Nothing special. Usually just a . . ."

"Hey, Sarge, pour a glass of your specialty. My tab. Ever had a Rummer, Jacko?"

"I don't think so."

"Good stuff. Kind of on-the-girl side but with a hint of the swashbuckler. Favorite here on The Bay. Especially the way Sarge makes it—who has yet to tell me his slight deviations in the mix."

"Sure. Thanks, Tony," Jack said. The bartender drew a Caribbean type glass and began to shoot various bottles into the mixer.

"It's the splash of Midori I throw that's extra. I've told Mr. Bledsloe that about a dozen times," the bartender explained to Jack. "Orange slice, sir?"

"Uh no, without is fine. Those fruit slices just get in the way. Why does he call you *Sarge?*"

"This is our local military hero," Tony interjected for him with just a hint of sarcasm that was almost untraceable. "He's up on The Hill. At that language school the army's got. Sarge here keeps us all updated on love and war, right, Sarge?"

"Sure, sir."

"You're a student there?" Jack asked.

"Yes sir."

"What language did they rope you with?"

"Czech."

"No kidding . . . you know, a long time ago I . . ."

"Anyway, Jack," Tony interrupted, sending the bartender back to his till. "You *have* been on the Monterey Net here, I'm afraid. Saw the blip in the weekly. That you bought the lot on Ocean View. Good location too, might I add. Also, that you're some sort of great inventor. What was it? The . . . hell, what did they call it?"

"Called the MAT. Cell phone piece. Guilty as charged. And I don't know about a great inventor. Just an inventor. And I have a partner who did half the work." He looked toward Sarge, who was immersed in cleaning glasses while picking up future gossip with his trained ear.

"Super, Jacko. That's just fantastic. You hear that, Sarge? We got a real inventor in our midst."

"So I hear, Mr. Bledsloe," he answered from the other end methodically. He came back down and extended his hand to Jack.

"They call me Sarge as Mr. Bledsloe said."

"Jack Strickland. As I was saying, I went to DLI up The Hill too. That was a bit of time ago though."

"You were an O, Mr. Strickland?" Sarge asked. "O" meaning the shortened connotation for officer.

"An officer? Hell no. I enlisted right out of high school. Navy. Stayed at the Foxtrot barracks, if it's still there. And it's Jack, Sarge."

"Jack it is, and those barracks are as well," he replied. Sarge pumped his hand with more sincerity the second time.

"Well, looks like we have two war heroes here," Tony added, slightly uncomfortably. Jack had for the moment almost forgotten him.

"So you're army, Sarge?"

"Yep."

"Staying in for the long haul?"

"Probably."

"How the hell do you have time to study Czech and work here? I don't remember having two minutes to spare between the school and the regular military bullshit."

"You do what you gotta do."

"Damn straight, Sarge," Jack replied. Tony ran a thumb up and down his glass. He gazed past Sarge, into the array of liqueurs. Presently, to his relief, two walked through the door. He waved with one arm and grabbed Jack's sleeve with the other.

"C'mon. Let's get a table and I'll introduce you. See you, Sarge," Tony said to the bartender who nodded his head curtly. "Miles!" he practically yelled. "What are you doing with my wife?"

"Scheming for her to take the better deal, Anthony, I'd say," the thin man who wore wire glasses jested back.

"Oh Tony, do try to behave just this once please," the woman on the man's arm stated with great exasperation. She was on the taller side, with long, brown hair, which exhibited intricate maintenance at least once a week at the salon, most likely time matched by the filing of her perfectly manicured nails. She wore an expensive vest and slacks, the outfit suggested in her demeanor that it was a pleasure and a chore to present. Dark eyes radiated a deep, scornful abyss, which had lured the opposite sex, since her early girlhood days, to fall off the precipice. Jack found her stunning.

"And who might this new friend be?" she asked. Her melodic voice climbed just an octave high enough to entice but not be subject of accusation.

"Miles, Drew," Tony stated magnificently as a ringmaster would orchestrate the bringing of the lions. "Allow me to introduce The Bay's newest inhabitant. One Mr. Jack Strickland. This is, although not particularly at the moment, my good wife, Drew, and my dear friend, Miles, who will be on probation if he doesn't get his paws off her."

"Hi," Jack said, making a round wave with his arm.

"He invented the MAT," Tony stated emphatically, this information sealing the introduction.

"Oh, *you're* the one. I read about that, of course. Some sort of phone thing. It's simply all Greek to me. Wasn't I just saying that the other day, Tony—about that inventor and how thank goodness men like him take their time to improve on things for the rest of us?"

"Yes, that's right, you surely did. We were at the coffee table," Tony agreed.

"Really, guys, it's no big deal," Jack said sheepishly. "Just a couple of regular engineers who stumbled on an idea. My partner gets most of the credit for the marketing. I'm no business genius. Just have a knack for putting things together."

"No big *deal*?" Drew smiled, showing perfectly whitened and aligned teeth. "Why, dear Jack, not everyone can just go and invent something, you know. Especially something grand. Can you imagine that, Tony? Just making something out of nothing?" she said, glancing sideways at her husband.

"No," Tony chuckled. "Too much time making a living at the company for me to contemplate."

"That's right, Drew. You'll have to forgive us lowly, regular folks at the daily grind," Miles added, shrugging his slender shoulders.

"Oh, boys, let's not get into all of that male I'm-on-top-of-the-mountain routine now, shall we? I am simply saying that some are meant to create, and what a luxury that one of those *someones* has decided to grace the rest of us with a product of his genius."

"How do you know it's good?" Jack asked wryly.

"Well, it simply *must* be, or you would not be here now, would you? My dear Jack. As I stated and emphatically believe, to work and succeed is well and noble, but to *create* out of the pure, thin air, why that simply gives me the *shivers*." She glanced toward her husband. "Have you ever invented anything, dear?"

"You never told me what you wanted, Drew," Tony answered. Jack was anxious to direct the conversation away from him. Drew put her hand toward her spouse's mouth before he could answer further.

"My lesser half has situated himself as the Vice President of Bledsloe Drywall," she said with great emphasis.

"No kidding?"

"Family company," Tony added. "Grandfather started it with a one shop building in Seaside, down the way."

"Seaside . . . just horrible, Jack. Nothing but dirty buildings and filthy people. Thank goodness the central location is in our own city district now. There really should be a prohibiting law from their entrance into our town. After all, they have their *own* side of The Bay." Drew folded her arms at the conclusion of the statement as if it permanently settled the matter.

"Filthy or not, that's where it started. And it *did* do well there as the area grew after WW II. But it was my father who really sent it on its way. Took one shop and expanded it to twenty-three outlets. From Seaside to San Jose."

"And now, the maestro here runs it," Miles said.

"Not yet, old boy," Tony replied. "Pop doesn't have the sense yet to retire. Wants to stick around a little longer, I suppose. But he will soon."

"In which my grand husband will be the *President* of Drywall," Drew said.

"Hail to the Chief," Miles added, raising his glass.

"And what's your line, Miles?" Jack asked.

"Public administration . . . for the city."

"Oh such men of false humility," Drew cried. "Miles is the District Liaison of Public Affairs. Appointed by the Mayor himself, years ago. Insuring that the tidy community of Monterey remains as so." She raised one finger in a wave to the server who placed drinks two tables down from them. The waitress came over promptly.

"Another round for the boys, please—and for myself. But just a touch of orange, not like your usual ones. Just a touch," she instructed, her voice scaling to the B sharp on the next octave. The girl, who looked to be about twenty-five, relayed the order in low tones to Sarge behind the cherry wood counter of the bar. He seemed to momentarily snicker out the side of his mouth.

Drew sighed. "I *do* hope they get it right. They never seem to get it right." Tony looked away as the silence ensued, common when entertaining a stranger. Finally, Jack focused back toward Miles, to the inaudible relief of the Bledsloes.

"So what does the District Liaison of Public Affairs do to keep Monterey tidy?"

"Oh, nothing terribly exciting, I'd say. Oversee committees mainly. You know, committees that decide which road project goes where so we don't have the tourists congesting the whole downtown up. Granting of licenses for city expositions. Everyone wants to have their expositions in Monterey. That sort of thing."

"Oh, the *tourists!*" Drew exacerbated abruptly. Several heads turned in the lounge. "My dear Jack has arrived in our city at the most inopportune time, I fear. They are just hither and thither. Late May to mid-September, I'm afraid. You have to reserve tables at the restaurants hours in advance. How am I to know what I wish to eat hours in advance? Isn't that so, Tony, my dear? Why just last weekend we tried to reserve at The Blue Dolphin on The Wharf. It was fully booked for the *entire* evening. During the season one cannot even get a decent meal. Never an adequate place to park either."

"We can get a decent meal, Drew. We just couldn't get one at The Dolphin that night," Tony argued.

"I'm simply *stating* that one would think that one wouldn't have to inform days in advance for the *luxury* of having a nice dinner at one of *our* restaurants. For Heaven's sake! I personally am *acquainted* with the owner. *Personally!*"

"They bring the money in though, if I remember correctly?" Jack noted.

"The tourists make the town, Drew," Miles stated. "Everyone knows that."

"Oh dear, I'm afraid I have committed a faux pas. My APOLOGIES, dear tourists!" She laughed and waved at the rest of the lounge who only stared at her. "We treasure them, of course," she continued, her voice amplified for effect on the heads, which had gone back to their drinks. She then lowered her tone as if to divulge a great detail, specifically tailored for them alone.

"Yes, boys, the tourists make the town. But it would be considerate of them to understand who *resides* in the town. We are the natives, after all."

"They probably feel we have access to The Bay all year long. So let them have their couple of months," Tony said. Drew threw up her hands as the waitress returned with the drinks.

"Hopeless with you boys. Absolutely hopeless." She took a small sip of her Rummer as a chef would test his sauce, and then wriggled her nose. "Well, not perfection, but this will do, I suppose," she stated just within earshot of the departing server.

Jack smiled. "So what do you do when you're not dining at The Blue Dolphin?"

Drew wagged a finger warningly. "Ah, clever boy, my dear Jack. I see you have already succumbed to my poor husband's influence. I am the Chairperson of one of Miles' grand committees. We deal with the advancement for equality in our region."

"What's that mean?"

"That means she loves homeless fags, Jack," Tony retorted.

"That is *not* what my committee represents," she replied with a small smile but slight glare in her eyes at her husband. "Please ignore him, dear Jack. Too many hours on that ridiculous tackle dummy in his wasteful years has dulled his senses, I fear. Our *organization* seeks fairness and tolerance on *all* levels in our community to creed, color *or* sexual disposition. We strive to bring our issues to the national level, of course."

"I thought we pretty much worked all that out in the sixties," Jack said, his smile slightly dissipating. From his roaming years, Jack had developed a common trait to many who spent their younger days venturing the world. And that attribute was the keen ability to sum up a person's character almost instantaneously. And the product of Drew's, in the course of the fifteen minutes he had known her, already began to irritate him. Even though a non-local, he had lived in Monterey before. At the bottom rung. And in that time, he didn't remember any organization battling for him.

"Oh no, Jack. No, no, not at all. Not at *all*," she prattled on. "Inequality exists on such a grand scale. Inequality, sexism and racism *exist*, Jack. It's all around you. I'm afraid it's a plague that has spread over the entire country."

"Maybe I have blinders on, but I don't see it," Jack answered. He wished the conversation would change. He could gather from her husband's silence and vacant stare out the window that he wished it would alter as well.

"Why, look up The Hill at that abominable school. The epitome of forced narrow-mindedness. Full of ruffians who just rampage our streets when the weekend arrives. Worse than the tourists."

"C'mon, Drew. Don't be so dramatic. They aren't rampaging, for Christ's sake. They go out like everyone else," Tony said.

"I believe I was stating my opinion, dear, which the last I recalled I was allowed to have. And my *opinion* is that these . . . these *people* are constantly doing nothing but looking for trouble in our town when they are allowed off of their precious hill. But, that is just my point of view, of course."

"Careful, Drew," Tony said. "Our new friend here was once a soldier."

"Sailor," Jack corrected. "And that was a long time ago."

"Oh, then you know, don't you, dear Jack? Of course you do, or you wouldn't have left the service, would you? Gone and made something of yourself. Created something," Drew concluded. "And may I ask how a man of your caliber ever ventured to join the *military* to begin with? You were not an officer, I gather?"

"No."

"Of course, being an officer is a tad better. Even I recognize that fact. But *enlisted* into the service? Whatever compelled you to do a thing like that, my dear Jack? Why did you not just go to college and become an engineer to begin with?"

"I was eighteen, out of high school and didn't have any money, Drew. A lot of guys in the exact same ship when I was in. One tour guys. Enlist, keep your nose clean for a few years, take the G.I. Bill and run when you get out."

"Dreadful. Simply dreadful. An example of why my organization, which my husband has such disdain for, exists. Having to subject poor young men to such . . . such *slavery*. Why they literally take your rights away, do they not? Starting with those frightful haircuts they give you. What exactly is the reason to demean someone like that?"

"Uniformity," Jack answered. "Always been that way. Kind of has to be. It *is* the military, Drew." Jack could see across the lounge that Sarge was wiping the same glass dry over and over while keenly listening to the entire conversation.

"Well, forgive me, Jack, but I do not see why there could not be an eenie-weenie bit of room for diversity in even the great Armed Forces. For example, let us take issue with the military's intolerance of homosexual soldiers. Did you know, Jack, my organization is actively, *actively* in the process of campaigning for openness without discrimination on that particular matter?"

"Oh God, here we go. Sorry, Jack," Tony groaned.

"There is no need to apologize for me, my dear. We are simply discussing a matter. You know the question of whether a soldier or a *sailor* can serve, based on his sexual *orientation* is of course simply silliness from a few old school dinosaurs, don't you, Jack?"

"Silliness? No, Drew, it is actually quite necessary. Especially on a ship."

"Oh come now, my dear Jack. Surely that is something they . . ."

"Drew, why don't you listen to him," her husband barked. "He was *in* for a few years, for God's sake."

"Do not shout, please. I can understand such matters without being a part of the actual entity, can I not? I can read. I can educate myself, can't I? Tony believes me to be quite ignorant, of course. But I am well-versed on the matter, Jack. *Well-versed*. I have spoken personally to a few high-ranking, ex-military personnel. Even from your navy."

"You've talked to a few homos in the entire military. You've never talked to the rest of them. The *huge* majority who thinks you're full of crap." Tony laughed at his own witticism and gulped a great portion of his drink down, returning his stare out the window.

"Tony, please, if you are not going to let me finish a simple thought . . . ." Drew clenched her cocktail napkin into a scrunched ball.

"Guys, guys," Jack intervened. "It's not worth fighting about. Look, Drew, all I'm saying is that on an aircraft carrier filled with a thousand sailors—mainly men, it's pretty essential that a harmony develops. There's no place to run off and take a time out when you're out to sea. Even women on board are a problem. Causes trouble with all the men, fair or not. You can't have problems for long or you'd have a mutiny on your hands. You have to get along. You work together, eat together and sleep together, usually bunched in a single room."

"Oh, Heavens," Drew interrupted. "But that's not what my friend, Lieutenant Parks, said. He had his own . . . "

He cut her off impatiently. "Officer. Officers get their own quarters—and even those are small quarters. But the majority of the crew, the majority who actually runs the ship—they're racked together, sometimes through fifteen-hour workdays. Like I said, even throw a woman in there, and it causes chaos. Like tossing an antelope into a pond filled with piranhas. Let someone come out of the closet in that type of environment. He'd mysteriously disappear over the rail one night on watch. Maybe it's not fair, but it's not fair that the majority of the crew, who *are* straight, have to worry about that guy checking you out in the shower. You wouldn't want to strip down in front of a bunch of sailors, would you, Drew?"

She reddened slightly as Tony's corner lip stifled a laugh. "But Jack, the military with all of its resources, could *accommodate*, could it not? Separate sleeping arrangements, showers and the like? The military should have an obligation to promote diversity among the ones who volunteer and . . . "

"Diversity?" Jack interrupted again. He rapidly grew weary of explaining hundreds of years of military protocol, which freed the world from tyranny twice in the last century. Sarge had stopped the façade of drying his glass and listened with obvious intent. "No, I disagree and so would anyone else in the service. All branches. The military's job is *not* to promote diversity. The military's job is to win wars. To do that it has to function as a unit. A harmonious unit, to get that particular mission done with the most efficiency. Everyone must be as one or it doesn't work. Even if sometimes things aren't *fair*. That's why some guys get brunt with crap from nitwits in charge. Because they can't destroy the order. They do that, the machine breaks down. And we lose wars. That's why they shave the heads the first day. Keeps the machine nice and lubed."

"Dreadful," Drew wailed.

"No, it's not dreadful. It's only hair. And it grows back. But they still keep it short for exactly that point. To remind you every time you look in the mirror that you're only a small cog in all of it. That you're not an individual. And you're not *diverse*. You're a unit. In fact, certain freedoms are taken away. One being that you can't just quit when you want. Like if a war starts. When your time is through, you can go back and be a long-haired-pothead-hippie, wearing pink bell-bottoms as far as they are concerned. They don't care what you were before or what you're going to be after. But while *in*, it's their way with no highway as a second option. If you don't like it, then don't sign up.

"But to create that chaotic type of environment you speak of—that *diversity*, which for some reason the military has been trying to create for about twenty years now, and you will destroy the essence of the military. Bending to civilian will. Bend to it, and wars will be lost in the end. Civilians who never served always have opinions based on a complete lack of knowledge of how the military actually runs. But, that's exactly what happens. Politicize the military and people die. And I'll bet the army opinion concurs. Hey, SARGE!" The bartender came over to the table.

"Now, let's not put poor Sarge on the spot, shall we?" Drew protested. She wished the discussion would alter course now as well.

"No, he'll be fine. Another branch of service. Tell us, Sarge. Settle a debate, even though I won't hold it against you that you're army green and all. How well would diversity work in your unit?"

"It doesn't," he answered. Seeing his purpose filled, he went back behind the counter and talked in low tones with the server.

"Thanks, Sarge," Jack called. Drew smiled brilliantly and clenched her drink. "Settled. Next round is on me. No hard feelings, Drew. Ok?"

"Of course not, my dear Jack. Why would there be hard feelings? We are all adults simply *discussing* things, are we not? I so much revel in the opinions that are not my own, you see? That's why we evolve, isn't it, boys?" Miles and Tony both grunted, indicating that, yes, this was indeed how they evolved. Jack, however, sensed a quiet tension between the couple as if Tony lived through him vicariously in the victory. On his third Rummer, he diplomatically changed the subject at last.

"So, Tony, Drew hints you played ball?"

"Oh yeah," Tony replied, relieved of the alteration. "Probably about the same time you were on that aircraft carrier. Wide receiver. Yale."

"Yale, really?"

"You bet, old boy. Majored in business so I'd have the credentials to take over Pop's company when he eases down. Didn't want the lowers to think he just gave it to me."

Did he get that 'old boy' he keeps calling everyone from Yale? Who does he think he is . . . Jay Gatsby? Jack thought.

"We all went east, of course, for college," Drew jumped in. "Brought back a bit of intelligentsia to California. That's where I met my Tony, at a Yale social. He was being scouted for the professional realm at the time, weren't you, dear?"

"No kidding?" Jack said.

"Yeah, way back when and all. It didn't work out," he explained, his eyes glancing to the window again.

"Now dear, not everyone even has a chance at the tryouts, do they? There is no dishonor in being dismissed at that level," Drew said.

"I wasn't dismissed, Drew, I was cut—after the first round," Tony explained irritably. "Probably for the better though, I suppose. Couldn't have run Pop's company if I was out wide and left."

"Still, I'm with your wife on that one. Pretty impressive," Jack said. Tony only shrugged.

Drew evidently was again ready to change topics. "You know where we should go? To Remmy's, downtown. It is via my social grapevine that they have a famous comedian performing there tonight. I simply love to laugh. I will gather that my dear Jack has never been to Remmy's?"

"Nope, just here for the second time. Haven't had time to walkabout much with the settling in and all."

"Oh, you simply *must* join us," she said. "Remmy's has popular entertainers all of the time who I've seen on television. Isn't it grand that we are such a haven for popular celebrities, Miles? California simply produces the most fantastic people."

"Sure is. Why they say Winona Ryder was in the city a month ago. Stayed right in the plaza for the weekend. What do you say about that, Jack? *Winona Ryder!*"

"I don't know, Miles. I don't really watch a lot of media," Jack answered. He instantly realized the social error with the silence that followed.

"Well then, let us be off. SARGE! My dear Sargie, you will call us a cab, won't you?" Drew said. Sarge nodded he would. He didn't point out their destination was a twenty minute walk away, and they could be there by the time the cab arrived. The group, slightly buzzing from the drinks, ambled out and thrust themselves by force into the Monterey night.

CHAPTER 2

It was an unusual 9:10 a.m. on Sunday when Jack awoke to a more unusual throbbing head from the night before. He slowly lumbered out of bed and felt the vague nausea that accompanied the headache. He squinted at the sun's rays, which came through his window. Last night's shirt was still on and his Dockers lay haphazardly strewn on the floor next to one of two shoes he had kicked off in two quick motions before he crashed into his bed.

After losing Miles to another native, Tony and Drew had taken Jack from Remmy's clichéd, comedic ensemble of California traffic and surgical implants, the response largely augmented by runs of coursing alcohol, to "Cello's." Jack had shared two bottles of wine at the Italian restaurant, followed by several more nightcaps at "Junior's Pub," just outside The Wharf while being dulled by several appetizers to counter the effect of the unusually high alcohol content coerced into his unsuspecting system. Tony and Drew had taken another cab home, but Jack insisted on walking back across the shoreline path to clear his head, which he did only to a small extent. It was 1:00 a.m. when they departed, Jack's only escort being a large black coffee in his hand. His head still spun when he reached his cove at the intersection of Fifth and Ocean View Blvd. He stood a few minutes and watched the night waves bring in the tide. Much akin to his youth, except that a younger Jack periodically frequented the six-pack on the shoreline in lieu of Merlot and Rum Runners.

The Bledsloes were to meet him this morning for breakfast. Drew quickly pointed out to Jack that it would actually be *brunch*. The café was just above The Row, where The Aquarium would open soon for the long lines of tourists, many of whom most likely would feel a kinship to Jack this morning. They were to meet at 11:00 a.m., if he recalled correctly, which gave him time to shower and coffee himself. He slumped on the counter in the bathroom, gazed into the mirror, began to lather his face, and then changed his mind and stepped directly into the shower. *Christ, who cares, you're not up in the barracks on The Hill anymore,* he thought. Besides, he would be prepped and starched tomorrow in several meetings in San Francisco with Everett and a few high level power types who manufactured their product en masse. He really didn't know why he polished himself much for that either. They didn't care if he came in a straw hat as long as they made money.

When he stepped out of his house, overcast clouds began to reel in the cold, characteristic to Monterey, where one hour a pair of shorts and sleeveless shirt would suffice, to be replaced the next by long pants and a jacket. When he arrived at the café, Drew was already there and waved impatiently for him to come over. She had a wine glass in her hand.

"Am I late?" he asked, knowing he wasn't.

"Oh no, my dear Jack. I'm very early," she answered, sipping on a white Chardonnay, which sat next to a dish of freshly cut strawberries. "I simply adore easing into the morning on Sundays."

"Where's Tony? Still not in bed recovering, I hope?"

"Tony?" she laughed. "Last night was just a *la vie* for one Mr. Bledsloe, I'm afraid. Has been since his Ivy days. Rummaging all night, two hours sleep and just as fresh as a daisy at six in the morning. He had an unexpected meeting with his dear father. He'll be along soon."

"Meeting?" Jack said. "Who the hell has a meeting on a Sunday?"

"Mr. Bledsloe Sr. I'm afraid there are no Sundays to that man. No Sundays, no holidays, just work and work. Not that I am complaining, you see, as the company has brought such good fortune to Tony and myself. And will bring more . . . in a few years." She leaned over and lowered her voice.

"Well, perhaps I am complaining, just a wee bit?" She laughed, and then motioned for the server. "Another glass for myself and one for Mr. Jack Strickland— he's an inventor and just arrived from . . . oh, Heavens! I cannot recall, Jack."

"Illinois."

"Of course . . . Illinois," she clarified for the server. Jack put up his hand, but Drew intervened.

"Oh yes, you must. Same for him please, no matter what he says. I fear we will have to instruct Mr. Strickland with all Monterey customs. And a lady shall not drink alone, especially when her husband abandons her for some infernal meeting." Jack was brought a glass of the same and a plate of strawberries as well. The first taste of the light wine made him queasy for a moment, which he attempted to conceal on his face. He was vastly improved by the second glass.

"So, my dear Jack, you were a strapping sailor long ago, were you?" she said mischievously.

"Oh no, not that again."

"Come, come now," Drew laughed lightly. "No political agendas just yet this morning. My head is still absolutely reeling from our adventurous outing last night with you incorrigible boys. Or was it this morning? I'm just ever so curious; how does a . . . navy man, is that correct?"

"Sure."

"How does a navy man become the inventor of such extravagance in our humble town?"

"It's not that extravagant," he explained. "It was a simple process, really. Long but simple. I went to school on the G.I. Bill after the navy, plus a bunch of money I saved on my own. While in the service, there were no room and board expenses. I got the engineering degree after the service. Then a friend and I got an idea. And it happened to sell."

"Your friend is in the area as well?"

"Everett? No way. Everett is a country boy through and through. I guess I am by root as well, being from a Mark Twain town in Illinois. He comes to the bay area in San Francisco for business only. Then goes back to his farm. Really, there isn't a lot for us to do. The product is sold. San Francisco mass produces and distributes it. We just look after the odds and ends mainly. Tweak the circuit design when needed. That sort of thing."

"Perhaps you should bring Everett here for all of us to meet," she implored.

"I don't know, Drew. He's not the type for bars and comedy routines. He has a family on the farm. Barbeques and beer for Everett," Jack chuckled but noticed the comment seemed to annoy Drew slightly. She sipped her glass, and then suddenly cornered him.

"And you, Mr. Jack Strickland, you're not . . . spoken for?" She began to show her teeth like a shark, before it chomps down on a mackerel.

"Nope."

"Oh, you don't get off that easily, do you think? Surely you have prospects? A man of your *stature* should have prospects, shouldn't he?"

"I think that's all the more reason to be wary," he said evenly. Jack was anxious to change the subject. "Speaking of, did Miles ever resurface?"

"That *man*. It is simply a wonder that I do tolerate him. Goes galloping off with every floozy impressed with Mr. District. Honestly, I do believe I have never seen a night through with Miles. He is formerly married, of course—twice. And every young local thinks she'll be little Miss Number Three."

"Oh," Jack replied. They sat in silence for several minutes, compensated by their wine.

"So, what about you and *Anthony?*" he asked.

"About?"

"How long have you two been together?"

"Hmmm," she sighed. "Together is a relative term, I'm afraid. We were *together* in our prodigal days in the east. The big games . . . they were always big games, Jack. You should have seen one Mr. Anthony Bledsloe at twenty-two. All the naïve of a still boy but the command of a General when he walked on the grass. Silly me. It isn't grass, of course. It's turf. The spongy, green turf the man-boys march on their way to primordial battle. Then to their women in victory or consolation. It was so Hemingway. I do miss it, do believe that I do. Tony, myself and several friends at the socials afterwards, with our espressos or whiskey teas to mock the cold outside. And even in the icy winds, the fire of schnapps that warmed our tummies, wrapped in our cloaks, walking back to the dormitories. Seeing the grand clock tower every night on our way home. Poor unfortunate me, Jack. I believe those days were the best of my life, if only I realized it at the time. . . . But Tony is the one to be mourned. We really believed he would continue to play professionally. He started every game in college. Of course, his coaches and managers reiterated it to him every day to the point where he thought the tryouts were nothing but a formality. An inconvenient few weeks until he would play as in college but without the tedious studies to distract him.

"Imagine being reinforced to greatness for years, and then quickly being dismissed, or *cut,* from the tryouts within weeks. The first round, Jack. They relieved him the very *first* round. Tony thought it was a mistake, of course. That they possibly mixed his number with another. They did not. He had already graduated.

So suddenly Anthony Bledsloe was not Tony, recognized by the entire campus as '42' on the back of his jersey. I still remember the number, Jack. He was transformed in one cruel phone call to ordinary Mr. Bledsloe. When they 'cut,' as you men say, with that call, they didn't cut a number. They removed part of his soul.

"And he had been so vibrant back then, Jack. My knight who galloped up with the dirtied jersey and bruised knees. Then he went to work for his father. And work he did, of course, trying to please that obstinate man who does not see fit to retire his company to his son. Mr. Bledsloe Sr. is sixty-eight for Heaven's sake. He has oodles of money. He should be traveling Europe. He should be on a Caribbean beach, sipping a Mai Tai or whatever he sips. If he were, my husband certainly wouldn't be late for our engagement on a *Sunday* morning. I believe he lingers on simply to torture poor Tony.

"But to answer your question, dear Jack, my Tony and I have been married for twelve years. How long we have been *together* is a matter of varied interpretations. But we tolerate it as a short means to a long end. Again, I'm certainly not complaining."

"Maybe just a wee bit," Jack taunted, causing Drew to laugh again and spill her glass slightly.

"Mr. Jack Strickland, such a novelty to our little community. Do tell me again what it was like on that little boat of yours in the navy?"

"Here we go again," he protested.

Drew put up her hand, flashing a large wedding diamond and several other rings. "Truce," she said. "For now, my dear Jack. I am simply *fascinated* with the military. All of that bellowing and marching around in polished shoes. And you really joined because you had nowhere else to go. How absolutely *romantic!* It reminds me of Melville's *Billy Budd* that I read my sophomore year."

"As I said, I joined up for the reason most of them join up. When you're eighteen and don't see a lot out there as a civilian. And I couldn't afford college."

"But your parents . . . " she began.

"My parents couldn't afford it either, Drew."

Her face flushed. "Oh my. You must think of me as an absolute snob."

"No, just from a different people," he answered. Drew sat quietly for a moment before she raised her head.

"And poor Sarge. Is that why he remains in the army?" she asked.

"Who Sarge? I doubt it. He looks older, maybe late twenties or even thirty. Probably on his third or even fourth enlistment. Some guys do stay in. A few even like it . . . . Not many though."

"Please forgive me, my dear Jack, but I do not see how anyone could *like* it. I've seen them running in little rows down The Hill. Why they absolutely *bark* at those boys."

"Well, Sarge has enough rank where he is probably the one doing the barking. The rest are a bunch of kids. Loud voices aren't going to hurt them any."

"If he is employed, why does he spend time working at Bully's, I wonder?"

"The service doesn't pay a lot, Drew . . . unless you're an officer. He probably has a wife and kids too." Her eyes narrowed.

"How much is not a lot?"

"Let's see. Seventeen years ago I cleared about nine hundred and fifty dollars a month as a newbie."

Drew sat back. "Nine hundred and fifty dollars, Jack? A *month?*"

"You understand room and board is thrown in for free."

"Even so! My room and board was 'thrown in' as well at college. Jack, my monthly stipend from father was almost twice that amount in my poor college days!" Jack sat silently for a moment and contemplated how much less of an endeavor getting through college would have been if he had almost two grand being sent from his father monthly. A cutting remark surfaced to his mind, which he suppressed with great difficulty as the woman across from him continued with an aghast expression on her face. He chose his words carefully as not to appear cloddish to his new acquaintance.

"I was young and single. Didn't need much. Bought a second-hand motorcycle to get around. Didn't drink a lot or gamble like the other squids. Clothes were even provided if I wanted to walk around in my duckies all day. That's a joke, Drew, I had regular clothes," Jack continued to explain as his face rose to crimson.

"My Jack, but it simply sounds so horrible!" Jack was to that point unaware it was as horrible as Drew believed as she sat and shook her head back and forth with sympathy.

"Not really." He was about to explain that in many ways it was just a job, no different than any other job, once accustomed to the strict regs, which accompanied it, when Tony entered through the door, gave a quick apologetic wave and sat next to his wife. He appeared as if he had just completed a mini-marathon.

"Goodman Jack, old boy. Pray, forgive the tardiness," he said in an accent, which Jack could not quite place.

"Oh really, dear, of course I've already excused you for him as I always do with these . . . unexpected circumstances." Tony eyed the almost empty wine glass.

"At it early I see." Drew leaned over to Jack as if to reveal a majestic secret and cupped her mouth but spoke loudly enough for several tables to overhear.

"Tony *greatly* concerns himself with wine before noon, you see. He is quite afraid that I may evolve into a societal lush."

"It's your liver I'm concerned with. Effect is harder on women than men," Tony answered briskly. "But I hate to be the killjoy. How about another glass of whatever they're having!" he yelled over to the counter.

"My dear," Drew said. "Jack was just educating me on the many facets of military life. It is simply fascinating."

"You're not starting that again, are you, Drew?" Tony warned.

"Oh, no need to worry. I keep all politically correct topics at bay until after the noon hour, dear."

"Thank God," her husband replied irritably.

"Anthony does not adhere to my volunteerism, you see, my dear Jack. A volunteer is likened to a slave, isn't that right, dear? Except even slaves had Sundays free."

"Drew, don't start."

"No, no," she started anyway, feeling the effects of the third glass of wine. "This housewife will stay complacent where she belongs, cleaning the kitchen, barefoot and pregnant."

"Our maids do some of the cooking and all the cleaning, Drew. For Christ's sake, you don't even grocery shop. Hey, Jack, did you know you can order groceries online? They deliver them right to your front door."

"No, I didn't know that," Jack said uncomfortably.

"Sure, there's a fee but what the hell when there's enough cash flow that you can afford to work on a committee for free. Ever ensuring Larry and Moe can happily marry each other, and all pets have access to a psychologist." Drew sat back angrily while Tony emptied half of his glass in one swish.

"Really, Drew," her husband continued. "If you want to keep advocating God for Gays the rest of your life, I really don't care. But you don't have to throw it on the dining room tablecloth every five minutes." The table sat quietly, the only sound was the distant splash of waves that hit the rocks on the shoreline.

"Why don't we order breakfast?" Jack suggested. They sat in silence and consumed poached eggs, home fried potatoes and blueberry pancakes while they switched from wine to juice. Once finished, Tony leaned back, his bulk brought the forward legs of the chair up several inches.

"Well, since we're already off the wagon, why don't we conjure up Miles at Bully's?" Tony said. Jack looked at his watch. *Christ, it's just past noon and I'm already buzzed.*

"I don't think so, guys. I have to be in San Francisco tomorrow and . . . "

"Nonsense, old boy." Tony jumped up, regaining his and Drew's humor at the thought of Sarge's Rummers. "We'll have Sarge make up a pitcher of his special blend. He works on Sundays. You like the Rummer, don't you, Jack?"

"Yeah, I have to admit that does sound tempting."

"Oh, you simply must go with us, my dear Jack. Rummers just past noon are so divine!" Drew rose, already tugging at his sleeve. They paid the check and eluded to walk the half-mile to freshen their heads. When they reached their destination, there were only two tables filled, most likely with tourists. Miles, as predicted, was at the end of the bar. He nursed a martini with two twists while reading the local paper.

"Miles!" Drew called. She let go of Jack and trotted to him. "Do tell, the prodigal companion has returned to us, I hope unharmed?"

"Safe and sound . . . for the most part," he replied.

"And where is the little harlot?"

"Safe and sound as well. I think so anyway."

Tony laughed. "I doubt it, old boy. Finish that swill so we can order some real drinks. Sarge!" he barked and gave a mock salute. "A pitcher of your finest mix." The bartender nodded and began the fusion of light and dark island rums with the many fruit juices.

"They really don't like that, Tony," Jack said under his breath.

"Like what?"

"That salute thing . . . from civilians."

"Oh hell, Jack, you're not going to get up in my ass too, now, are you? Christ, he works here."

"I'm just saying . . . " Jack began as Tony left toward the high table in the corner. The rest followed. A few minutes later the pitcher was brought over.

"Sarge, Jack here says you don't like salutes from us civilians. That true?"

"You know where the salute comes from, Mr. Bledsloe?" he asked, placing the pitcher in front of him. His face showed he was not sharing the frivolity as Jack grew quiet.

"I don't know, something like some general way back when . . . "

"No," the man cut him off sharply. "Nothing to do with a general. The *salute*, some believe, came during the days of knighthood. Two passersby, no correction, two *knights* would gallop by, each lifting the face mask off his helmet. A sign to each that the other was friend, not foe. Others think it came from Roman history. A subordinate soldier would raise his hand to feign off the shine, which radiated from his superior's eyes. In our own history, our *warriors* hold the tradition as well. Enlisted men raise their outstretched fingers to the corner of the eye. At a forty-five degree angle. Not fifty degrees. Not forty degrees. *Forty-five.* And lower-ranking officers raise the protocol to higher-ranking officers. Lower rank first. Except if one is wearing a Congressional Medal of Honor, in which case the Medal is saluted first regardless of the rank. Civilians often ask what all of this protocol has to do with soldiering. The answer is it has nothing to do with soldiering. It has to do with honoring the dead who stood by the rank structure—officers and enlisted. Same reason we press uniforms and keep shoes polished in garrison. For the dead. And we salute to honor our flag as well." The table sat silent as Jack bit down on his lip to refrain from smirking at Tony, whose face blushed slightly red.

"Well, Sarge," Drew implored. "Whatever are we civilians to do then?"

"You don't, Mrs. Bledsloe. A civilian holds his or her hand over the heart. Like the Pledge of Allegiance at school. The business of saluting is better left to us soldier types. Enjoy the Rummers," he said. He returned to the bar.

"Touchy bastard today," Tony said in a quiet tone. "Not my fault he's working on Sunday."

"You hit a nerve there, Tony," Jack replied.

"I'll tip him out extra and he'll be fine."

"I simply detest it when he goes on with that *Mrs. Bledsloe* stuff," Drew added.

They sat and drank their Rummers. A second pitcher was ordered shortly after. Then another. By the time they finished, it was late afternoon. Jack took a walk, leaving the group, and stopped at "Luigi's" on his way home. He ordered the pasta primavera and a large beer to the mixed rums, which coursed in his system. Another one followed after the meal. He reasoned he had already set himself up for a miserable hangover the next morning, so proposed he might as well complete the job and pay in full in San Francisco's traffic tomorrow. Upon reaching his home at 8:00 p.m., he popped two more from his fridge before Jack finally settled down into what became a dreamless sleep.

CHAPTER 3

Jack's drive to San Francisco did indeed prove arduous. He had awakened several times during the night with dehydration headaches until the alarm finally called him at 5:15 a.m. Normally, he never drank before a workday, even in his seaman years he avoided the small galley bars on the ship unless he knew for certain that he wasn't about to face another twelve-hour shift in the immediate a.m. Jack knew many who chose to forgo that particular philosophy. They looked like a constant state of decay the next morning, counting the hours in-between popping aspirin, Mountain Dews and pots of coffee until they could once again consume the numbing potion, which rendered a temporary state of amnesia for who and what they were. His lack of development of this habit had gotten him through engineering school and later had allowed his nights to be consumed with a different outlet, which had led to his industry.

However, in lieu of this custom was his recent encounter with the Bledsloes. Also, there was now another factor. For the first time in his still relatively young life, Jack Strickland was bored. Nineteen to twenty-two had flown by after his graduation from the Russian Basic Course on top of The Hill. The next four years, Jack barely left the room in a shared house with three other engineering students; two who did not graduate with the degree because they left their desks too often. There had been only intermittent girlfriends. After completing his degree, he had met Everett at the company. Then, after three years of intense work learning his craft while at the same time producing the MAT, Jack had woken up one day to realize his twenties had somehow escaped him. Time, the immeasurable price, paid in years for success. And paid in full, almost two decades from the day he stood at the processing center with right arm acutely raised at the age of eighteen, he suddenly found himself an unexpected multimillionaire. No morning time card to punch, his product eaten and digesting well in the stomach of a monster conglomerate, which spewed out Jack and Everett's royalties at the other end.

In four months he would be thirty-six. His house was paid in full, and his few remaining millions were in the bank at a conservative interest. The corporation that produced the device in San Francisco met with Jack and Everett frequently for reimbursed consultations, but in reality, between conference calls and modifications, the workload really only consumed about fifteen hours a week. The highly compensated meetings were contracted but for appearances' sake only. Jack could probably stretch out on the shoreline next to his cove with one of Sarge's Rummers for the rest of his life, and no one would care.

Jack Strickland neither liked nor disliked high society people and remained quite ignorant that he was now one of them, whether he admitted it vocally or not. Old Monterey was sixteen years past, in which he could not afford one night a month in entertainment of what he paid for two consecutive days in New Monterey. In his New Monterey, he could afford it every night.

Which he thought about a great deal during the two hour grind that slowly turned his wheels on Highway 101, en route to the outskirts of the city. From there, he would park and take the polished BART railway, which would finally drop him in the downtown by 9:00 a.m. He would catch a café near the conference building. And again on the way back. Jack slowly became accustomed to eating out every meal. And why not? The brunch restaurant, where he had gone yesterday with Tony and Drew, could make a Denver omelet and hash browns with far more culinary skill than he possessed. And he had a plethora of choices for lunch and dinner between The Wharf, The Row and downtown Monterey. He had stocked his refrigerator when he moved in and barely touched its contents since. Gradually, it occurred to him that he was wealthy. If he didn't wish, he would never have to open his fridge door again. Two hundred and fifty dollars a day on restaurants, coffee shops and bars wouldn't even make a dent in his fortune.

And the Bledsloes and Miles were fun too, although he sensed a tension between Drew and her husband. But he imagined that element existed in all couples who had tied the sheepshank for over a decade, the knot so hardened that it would be impossible to undo. Tony had money, old and new, coming in. Jack had looked up his father's company on the internet the other night. Tony might not be a multimillionaire, but he probably reeled in more than a few hundred thousand a year. Plus profit sharing during the good quarters. And when his dad did retire, it was certain that Tony would become a multimillionaire quickly after. So why did he care if Drew spent her time around a bunch of flamers anyway?

He remembered his navy days as his car started and stopped on the dewy pavement with horns vainly blaring in the background. Even though in Intelligence, a sailor was a sailor as a soldier was a soldier and a marine a marine. He belonged to that club and the officers belonged to the smaller but far more prestigious other. On the ship, his fellow members were vulgar men who pursued hard drinking, gambling and cohorts in Singapore's darker light districts. In contrast, this novel refinement, which now encompassed Jack, pleased him. Besides, was it that much of an unpardonable sin to indulge in a little spirit on Sunday—even if that little was actually a lot? Jack believed it was secure to acknowledge that in Tony, Miles and Drew he was in the company of friends.

When he arrived at the parking garage, Jack walked across the street and purchased a ticket at the steel enclosed stand, which represented the Bay Area Rapid Transit or commonly known as BART, San Francisco's dear friend to commuters. He had a deli sandwich while he waited for the train, his stomach first protested, and then finally surrendered to the badly needed nutrients.

Everett had flown in last night and waited for him and the others in the conference room. "You alright, Jack? You look a bit under the rain cloud," he said.

"Late night . . . . Met a few hard chargers."

"In Monterey?"

"Yeah, alright people, but they do know how to night life."

"I bet. Lot of rich folks in Monterey."

"Everett, we are one of those rich folks now," Jack replied. His friend entirely missed the sarcastic tone.

"True, but the difference is we weren't always so."

"Yeah, I guess. So you find anything changed around you since the Fortune 500 article?"

"Nope," Everett said flatly. He scrunched his eyebrows, a telltale sign that he was pondering after the fact. "Well, some things, I reckon. I run the farm still but have a lot more paid help these days." Everett had a generational plot of land bestowed upon him prior to his engineering life. He had managed engineering school in the winter months and believed a high paying job would be a good backup for the rainy days, which in the farming industry meant the seasons it didn't profit or when one of nature's little bugs decided to buffet on the crop all summer. Although a yearly harvest meant financially little to Everett these days, by force of genetic habit, he continued to grow and deemed it an added blessing that he could give jobs, badly needed in the poor region, to others.

The secretary came in with more coffee and explained hurriedly that the associates were running late in a previous meeting and would be in within a few minutes.

"No problem," Jack said. "Just gives us a little more time to catch up." Jack described the Bledsloes to Everett, taking the entire cup to accomplish the task.

"She doesn't work or tend house? Really?" Everett marveled at the account of Tony's wife.

"Apparently not. She does this volunteer thing. Obsessed with it, actually. Minority rights, gay rights, cats' rights, you know—typical California philosophy."

"Bunch of socialists out here," Everett confirmed.

"Oh, I don't know. I don't think Drew is a communist or anything. Just a lot of time on her hands."

"That's what I mean, Jack. Always interesting how the intellects *have* so much time to solve everyone's problems, especially when they don't have a job. I knew those types in college. Always the same class that didn't pay for their school or rent. Idealistic. They field in easy majors, which gave them plenty of time for protests and activism." Jack laughed at the cynicism.

"No, really," Everett continued. "I knew one in particular when I was a junior level student. Studying thermodynamics. Remember the thermo days?"

"Oh Christ, yeah—proudest C I ever got," Jack replied.

"Exactly. Well, this Molly or Polly or whatever handle she carried was in one of my electives. Philosophy. God, I hated philosophy. Since it was either that or another feel good course just like it, I stayed on. But Molly or Polly, she *loved* it. Talked all the time about these guys. Descartes, Nietzsche and whoever else the heck they talk about. I didn't have much regard for a bunch of dead thinkers. I had problem formulas that took three days to solve. She was an avid communist too. Actually proud of the fact as if it made her smarts better to everyone else around her. I was like: *No shiola, Sherlock, I bet you do duck with the commies when you're majoring in something that isn't that hard and not going to make you a lot of money.* Unless you get a doctorate and write books for the other philo junkies, but well, that takes some work too. So you got about two choices when you're in college, the way I see it. You get a power degree like medical or engineering and sweat blood for years or get an easier one, and then sweat blood for years working your way up the company ladder. But there ain't no other way you're going to get it. Those two forks in the road circle back to the same end point.

"But she didn't want to *do* that. No sir. She wanted to tell me every other day how it wasn't fair that us engineers and medical people started out so high and everyone else didn't. System wasn't just and all that shiola. Never mind those three-day problems I had to solve to pass the coursework. Just not fair to her and all. Everyone should be equal whether they performed equally or not. Had all sorts of time to *think about things* in her coffee shops. She didn't have three-day problems. Asked me once to meet *her* people. I assumed they were a bunch of Reds as well."

"Did you?" Jack asked.

"Heck no, I was studying thermodynamics, remember? Point is, she'll go through life madder than a clipped hornet because she's not making what an engineer makes. Probably be furious that I made the million mark too—not that she spent long nights modifying the MAT."

"Hear, hear," Jack applauded, raising his cup.

"That's what this Drew sounds like to me, buddy. Except she doesn't have any reason to be mad at all. And I'll bet one hen egg she's a looker too."

"Gorgeous is more the word. Even at thirty-something." Jack had finally said it out loud. Drew was pretty. Drew was gorgeous. Drew could get anything she wanted with pretty and gorgeous.

"Right. And she went to college being a looker, looking for some future C.E.O. And it sounds like she got one. So now she can sit around and think about things too . . . just like my little friend from philosophy. But the rich ones, they're the worst kind. Kind that's got money never earned and still thinks their opinion of how the rest of us should be matters one iota."

"Pretty harsh synopsis, Everett," Jack said but smiled slightly at the insight. The fact was Everett had never even met the woman, however, so far was pretty much right on target from Jack's unspoken analysis as well. "How about Shirley though? She still tends the house?"

"Yep. Cooks too. I brought up bringing help around once, about a year ago. She almost hit me with the fryer. No stranger was going to come into her house and start meddlin' around, let me tell you that—money or no money. No sir. I take her and the kids out a lot more now, but don't even think you're going to tell my gal someone else is going to run her domain, even on the part-time. Bet your new pals don't even have children."

"I don't think so . . . . At least they never mentioned any. Can't see how with the way they run around every night," Jack noted.

"Of course not. Probably too inconvenient for your Miss Daisy Drew. Watch yourself out there, Jack. I mean, like I said, you're a member of the money club now. There are women who make it a profession going after rich guys. Then when these guys come back to planet earth a few years later, they realize two things. One, their little cutie is spending every cent they got, and *two*, divorce will cost them half of everything anyway. When those two things come together in their minds that's when they realize they just bought a caseload of screwed."

"C'mon, Everett, they can't all be like that."

"All I'm saying is be careful, Jack. You and I are new at this and don't have all the high society street smarts yet. Like our old conservative friend once said. Trust . . . but *verify*."

Jack laughed again as the thick mahogany doors opened and four principals walked in with leather briefcases in hand. Jack decided to stay in San Francisco over the night after the prolonged meetings, which lasted several hours longer than he anticipated. Later that evening, he had his prior customary two beers at the bar as he and his colleague talked of lighter topics concerning sports and Everett's family.

CHAPTER 4

When he returned to Monterey early the next afternoon, Jack found himself more at his usual par. A day of high-level meetings with Everett proved to be far less taxing to his physiology than a night with the Bledsloes. He convinced Everett at some point the previous evening to come down to Monterey sometime to at least show him The Bay properly.

Jack had muddled through the two hours of traffic back, finding Highway 101, which turned into the infamous Route 1 that could take a traveler through the high cliffs of the Big Sur region, to the low beaches of San Simeon, and then Morro Bay. He drove through the rolling sands of Marina, which indicated that Monterey was only a few miles further, past the now closed Fort Ord and Reservation Drive, a street of hotels and once haven for 7th Infantry soldiers on pass. He finally exited off Del Monte, which would take him to the shoreline path. It was after 2:00 p.m. when he opened his door. He dropped his briefcase on the sofa and didn't plan on retrieving it until late tomorrow. Then he changed out of his three-piece suit quickly as Jack always did when arriving home. He never quite understood the logic of a garment, whose sole function consisted of making the wearer uncomfortable all day long. He opted for his more preferred blue jeans, sock free loafers and a gray polo with short sleeves.

As he sat on the other end from his abandoned case, he pinched the remote to his large widescreen, flipped through its grandness and acutely realized there was nothing notable on. He fidgeted a bit in the large, quiet house, and then looked out the window toward the surf.

"Why not?" he muttered to himself. Jack grabbed his lightweight jacket and an old baseball cap, which clearly stated the reign of the Cubs was bound and coming. He exited again toward the shoreline path. When he arrived at Bully's, Tony and Miles were at a table with a binder between them as well as a pitcher of

Rummers. Sarge, upon seeing him, gave a wave, causing the woman at the bar to spin around. She rapidly waved him over as well.

"Leave the boys alone, my dear Jack, and do sit by me. They are quite absorbed at the moment."

"Go on over, Jack," Tony bellowed across the lounge. "Just give us a few, old boy, ok?" Jack nodded and took the bar stool as Tony and Miles hunched themselves over the papers and stole to quiet voices again.

"My Jack," Drew said, planting a kiss on his cheek. "And where did you hide yourself last night?"

"I stayed over. Longer meeting than I thought. Way longer, actually. And I didn't feel like the traffic twice in one day."

"Oh lovely San Francisco! Such a delightful city. Such *progression* in culture. We in Monterey like to imagine San Fran as our big sister role model."

"Like I said, lot of traffic though."

"Oh, my dear Jack, what are we going to *do* with you? Our small-town boy transplanted to California!" Jack reasoned Drew to be on her second or third beverage, indicative from the high shrill in her voice common to all women on their second or third beverage. "However . . . I am simply *thrilled* that you stopped by to visit us today. We were just speaking of our little . . . . Sargie, my dear Jack is with empty glass . . . thank you, dear Sarge." She poured the mixture for Jack. "Now what was I saying?" she giggled.

"Your little something," he replied, tasting the rum and raspberry.

"YES! Our end of summer get-together. Not for some time, of course. Always the second weekend of September. Our toast to the tourist leave. Always, my dear Jack. And you must join us. You will join us, won't you, Jack?"

"Sure . . . thanks. Let me know and I'll be there." Drew grabbed his neck and brought him closer. Jack reddened and cast a glance at Tony who seemed to remain intrigued in whatever he and Miles were discussing.

"And speaking of social engagements, there is someone I simply must introduce you to soon."

"Uh oh," Jack said. He smiled as a greater flush stole further.

"Now, now, my dear Jack, no schoolboy antics with *ma amie*. I certainly would not mix and match just anyone like those . . . well, you know those types of women I am sure. Beverly is a magnificent persona. Simply *bravura!* She would be thrilled to meet you, I am certain. You just leave the matter all up to your Drew." She tapped him on the forehead with her red painted nail.

"Ok, sounds fine, Drew," Jack replied, trying to appear blasé and failing. The deepening rose smolder had migrated from his neck to his entire face as well.

"We're done, Drew, so take your paws off Jack and come on over!" Tony shouted to the bar. "Where were you last night, old boy? Thought we had scared you off for good."

"San Francisco. Long meeting. You know how those go," he explained, feeling the need to reiterate the fact.

"Christ, do I."

"I was just telling Jack how much I adore San Francisco. That's where I go to shop for all of my clothes. People in New York always think they are the first. You always hear New York this and New York that, for Heaven's sake. But I believe that one can always trace the root of high fashion to the *West* Coast. Then you hear about New York. Then it seeps to the rest of the country, always well after it has concluded here. How silly the rest of the country looks. Wearing their outdated costumes. They purchase these articles in their own towns thinking they are *tres chic* with Monterey or New York and oops—they are a year late."

"Maybe they don't care, Drew," Tony said.

"I simply cannot imagine how one does not care about personal appearance, my love. The ensemble makes a person, of course. Oh, you deem me as superficial, but I'm not. It's simply a matter of taste. How seriously would we take the President if he shopped the Goodwill store? Not very, mind you. Not very at all." Tony muttered something, but then scrunched his eyebrows and thought better of it. It was his extensive experience that picking a battle such as this would be costly for his troops for little ground gained. Without subtlety, he changed the subject.

"You told him about the end of summer, right?" he asked.

"*Of course* I told him, dear. And Jack has informed me that he will indeed honor the Bledsloe chateau with his presence."

"The Bledsloe's get-togethers are always a hit, Jack. If you're not hitting the floor by morning," Miles said. "You'll get to meet the real movers in Monterey. Will the mayor be there this year, Drew?"

"Oh, Alex will come by, I am certain," she answered with a wink to Jack, which he nodded in understanding in which he did not.

"So it's Alex? You and the mayor are that tight?" Jack asked.

"We know a lot of people, old boy," Tony said. "As I have stated, my company, or should I say my father's, has been centrally located in the city for two generations. We've built up a lot of volume in all those years, Jack. A lot of volume. Type of volume where you better know the right people to keep John Q Bureaucrat off your back."

"What bureaucrats?"

"Oh, you know," Tony answered, taking another long slug from his glass. "Bureaucrats. Squinty-eyed little desk jockeys who have nothing better to do with their lives. Safety inspectors. Auditors. Type of guys who sat in the stands wishing they could play in the real game. They didn't so they get their little certifications and spend the rest of their piss ant lives taking it out on everyone they can. Bunch of little yap dogs waiting to be released. But they *are* controlled. By the upper echelon.

"Let me tell you about business, Jack, and take no offense, old boy, but you've got a pretty good gig going. Invent something, and then sell it. Let a corporation handle all the headache. Hell, I wish I could have done that because I got the headache part. When you own the company, it's different. Altogether different. You're part of the community. Now, no one gives two cents' worth of damn about the mechanic shop on the corner. What's he going to do? Pay his rent for the block and fix cars and nobody really gives a shit about him. He can be replaced by the next grease monkey from voc-tech. Who cares? I'm talking a *business*. Something that employs, say, a few hundred or thousand natives. Something that contributes significant tax revenues to the town. Now you're in the mix with that kind of steam. Your contacts aren't wherever Joe's Garage hangs out after work in their oil stained overalls, slurping Budweiser. Your contacts are city council members. And *other* city officials."

"Like the mayor," Jack said.

"Like the mayor. Now, let's look at that for a minute, old boy. You're schmoozing around with the gatekeepers to the kennel of all those hungry yappers. You piss one of them off and up goes the gate and hounds released. Try to be some radical businessman in this town. They'll run you out in a month. Oh, they'll do it legal—bet on that one. Backed by the town's heavy hitters in the district. Take the head Safety Inspector here. What's his name, Drew?"

"Maxwell Brogan is who you're talking about, Tony," Miles said.

"Right. Good old Max. Friend by day and royal pain in the ass at night if he wants to be. Max slinks into corporate establishments with a book that's about four hundred pages long. His regulation book. You'd think it was his goddamn Bible. All he has to do is go through it and find a violation somewhere. Even though everyone knows that no company can follow *every* reg all the time, for Christ's sake. And Max knows it too. So the businesses that get along, walk along and the ones that don't . . . . They don't walk at all."

"Seriously?" Jack asked.

"You bet, old boy," Tony continued. "Let me tell you a Monterey fable. About ten years ago this couple slouches in with their shop. Some low-level, bullshit bar near The Wharf, bought with an inheritance of some sort. They try to undercut everyone else, lowering drink prices to the point where the wrong element starts coming in. The kind of element we don't want. This is a nice, upscale tourist town, Jack. We don't need a bunch of hard drinking Archie Bunkers here. Bad enough with the joes who come down from The Hill on weekends."

"Of course, we don't mean you, Jack," Drew added diplomatically as Jack nodded slowly.

"He knows we don't mean him. I'm talking about . . . well, you know. Anyway, a few city council members try to go talk to the owner of the place. They went down real polite, trying to be nice to the guy, for Christ's sake. Explained this was a clean town, and we don't need stained collars from all over Seaside, staggering out of his bar drunk every Friday and Saturday night in sight of The Wharf."

"Were they doing that, Tony?" Jack asked.

"No . . . no, let me finish. They weren't *yet*. But give it time and they would be. Start giving two for ones at low prices for that piss vinegar they drink and they would be pretty soon. I can guarantee you that, old boy. So they suggest that if he upped his prices and kept the place classed, the boys from Joe's Garage wouldn't be there in their filthy jumpsuits. If I know one thing, I know *that* type isn't paying five bucks for a beer. Hell, he'd make way more money. In case you haven't noticed, there are more than a few tourists in town during the summer. Every summer. He'd have made a fortune like the rest of us. Christ, they were trying to *help* the stupid schmuck.

"But no, the guy won't budge. Has this working class hero mentality, going to stick it in the town's face, whether we like it or not. Damn near threw those councilmen out of his bar. *Councilmen,* for Christ's sake. So about a couple of months later, the fire marshal shows up unannounced at Mr.Working Class' place. Then a few undercovers from the A.T.F. Found the same regs broken that you'd find in Bully's any given night of the week. You know, an underage who slipped through or something. Difference was Bully's didn't piss on the councilmen. Place was shut down shortly after."

"And that *horrible* man took his rubble out of Monterey," Drew added victoriously.

"Doesn't sound very capitalistic," Jack said.

"Free market isn't as free as you think," Miles replied with another wink to him.

"Which is why we keep dear, womanizing Miles around at all," Drew said, rubbing his neck. "He is one of our safety nets, aren't you, Miles?"

"I see," Jack said.

"It's not like illegal stuff. Drywall equals construction. Construction equals regs. That's what we were chatting about a few minutes ago," Tony added with a touch of defensiveness. "Just a matter of knowing who to know really. We scratch their backs, and they keep the flies off ours." They drained their glasses and ordered another pitcher. Light music played in the background as the flames from the fuel supplied lounge fire in the center made Jack drowsy. As the others seemed to be invigorated by the continuous flow of Sarge's rum blend, he began to nod off, catching only small particles from Drew's conversation, which seemed to be unremitting. He finished one more glass, and then got up.

"Sorry, guys, have to call it a night," he said with a yawn as confirmation.

"Do come by Saturday night, dear Jack," Drew said mischievously. "I do have someone you simply must be introduced to."

"Ok," he replied. He reddened again at the crooked grins of Miles and Tony. Thus assured that he would indeed be present Saturday, Jack walked out once more with a spinning head, his face met by the cool breeze from The Bay. He strolled toward the shoreline path. *I'm doing too much of this. Too much booze.* He didn't drink like this normally, even in the military. His reasoning as he walked along the sounds of night waves, which crashed into the rocks, dictated that in the military he had a purpose to achieve. Achieving fluency in Russian in one year is not an easy task. And neither was obtaining an engineering degree after his time in service. And now he was different. Something had changed and not by token of his bank account either. For the first time since he was eighteen, he had nothing to drive toward. Almost as if the great success came too early in his life. He felt . . . .

Stagnant

Of course he did. *Similar to winning the gold medal in the Olympics,* he thought. *You push and force yourself to the limits for years. Sacrificing time, sleep, friends and life. For the one ultimate objective. Then what happens once you reach the frozen summit? Sit around and make advertisements for snow cones.* Something else bothered him as he ambled to his house with a steaming coffee in the night air. Tony's story about the bar years ago had disturbed him. The entire narrative seemed a slap in the face to free enterprise. And the comment on an auto shop at the corner. A mechanic not viewed as a real businessman—in their eyes. His dad was good friends with the town mechanic from his hometown in Illinois. Happened to be a hell of a nice guy. *They wouldn't be bitching about greasy overalls if their car wasn't running.* He counted himself lucky he invented the MAT instead of opening a bar, like that couple Tony talked about years ago. And what if he was a small shop owner? *How'd they treat me, I wonder? If I even got close enough to them to be treated at all.*

These thoughts swirled with the rum through Jack's head as he fell asleep on the couch with his shoes and television still on.

CHAPTER 5

June

Jack showed up Saturday at Bully's at 6:00 p.m., about two hours before the lounge would fill with regulars and tourists. The restaurants' various aromas of seafood and grill drifted across the water and blended with the salty pungent scents of floating kelp from the sea as day Monterey would transcend into the weekend night life. He was dressed smartly, yet casual, a local habit already incarnated into his subconscious. He arrived earlier than the Bledsloes as to give the impression that he was there only by happenstance, even as it was grossly understood that he was not. This gave him the amused thought of the extent people go to, when attempting to date, to give the appearance that they aren't. He went to the bar and stood at the end. Sarge gave him a wave and came over a moment later.

"Jack, how goes it tonight?"

"Oh, you know, the usual."

"So, you drinking the usual as well?"

"How about just a beer? Whatever light wheat you have," Jack said.

"There you go. You don't strike me as the Rummer type anyway," the bartender replied, pulling a glass. Jack tipped a dollar over custom and started for the near empty lounge.

"Think I'll get a window seat tonight," he said nonchalantly.

"Sure, Jack. Just wave for the refill."

"Thanks, Sarge. See you later."

He was nursing the domestic lager slowly, not wishing to be tipsy when Drew brought in whatever her name was. The antidote also served to calm the fluttering nerves in his stomach. He hadn't socialized much in the last few years. Contrary to what everyone thought, in-between the creation and marketing of his product, there had not been a great deal of time to even think about the prospect.

The notion had still not occurred to Jack that he was incredibly rich, even by the standards of his locality. He wasn't a millionaire but a *multimillionaire.* The fact of his elevated accessibility had not come to full realization concerning the opposite sex.

At close to 8:00 p.m., they arrived. Jack almost choked mid-gulp into the second lager. He had never been a thrilling fan of myopic encounters, proven in his past that such an encounter was comprised of one who couldn't manage on her own. Usually from a deficit in the superficiality department. Drew's friend was not deficient in this particular category. She was absolutely stunning with flowing auburn hair and a figure, which could easily take a stroll down any runway. Drew pointed to him from the entrance and walked her friend over as Tony stopped to chat with another couple who sat at one of the high tables.

"Jack Strickland, this is my dearest friend, Beverly Laubauch," she announced as they sat. "He's the one I told you about. Monterey's greatest inventor."

"I don't know about that," he said, trying to stand before they sat down. "Like I keep saying, just an engineer with an idea. Nice to meet you, Beverly." He tried to invoke casualness into his voice, which failed as always does when forced. She seemed not to notice, her hazel eyes staring directly into his.

"Well, it's nice to meet you too, Jack Strickland," she said, scooting her chair closer to his. "Drew has just raved about you." Jack flushed and tried to think of a witty remark when Tony saved him by stepping to the table.

"Sorry," he said. "So everyone has met everyone, thus relieving me of the honors?"

"We've met—and then some," Beverly replied slyly without breaking her gaze.

"Good. What the hell is that you're swilling, old boy? Sarge! How about a pitcher of the usual bird!" Sarge nodded from the bar and began the mix.

"Going to be one of those nights, I see."

"What night isn't, Jacko," Tony replied. Jack was grateful he had taken the two lagers prior. He felt just relaxed enough to attempt charm but not stupidly intoxicated. He mentally reminded himself to keep it that way. But they consumed the pitcher faster than he had hoped for with Tony egging him to keep pace. Drew acted as conductor, finding new compositions of thought when the music lulled between Jack and Beverly, and kept the melody continuous. At the bottom of the second batch of Rummers, Tony snapped his fingers toward the now busy bar, when Drew interrupted.

"Hold it a wee second, would you, dear?" She leaned toward the three. "Do you know what would be absolutely divine right this moment?" They stared, indicating they did not have the foggiest.

"Cello's specialty Merlot. Jack, they have a Merlot from Sonoma, which is simply exquisite, and I am just in the mind for exquisite wine tonight. Shall we?" Drew asked, already putting on her coat. Beverly followed suit as the men went to the bar.

"I got the tab," Jack said and pulled a hundred bill from his wallet.

"Not necessary, old boy," Tony protested.

"That's ok. I'm having a pretty good time."

Tony laughed softly. "And bound to get better from the looks of it, Jacko. She likes you."

"Think so?"

"She wouldn't have come with Drew if she wasn't interested," Tony replied as Jack's brow furrowed.

"She's never met me though."

Tony chuckled sarcastically. "Welcome to the land of the haves, Mr. Strickland. *With* all the bennies." Jack laughed, not certain why and not overly concerned with the fact. The mixture gave him a warm sensation, heated more by the gorgeous woman he was entertaining who seemed to have taken instant affect to him. And frankly, he wasn't going to analyze why at this particular moment.

At Cello's, they had appetizers and three bottles of the Merlot, which Drew spoke of. By the end of the evening, Jack realized he had spent three hundred dollars on the date. He had no worry of the amount, however, as Beverly seemed to have migrated closer to him throughout the course of the night while making a new habit of rubbing his shoulder several times. The restaurant began to empty as the busboys, probably from Seaside, collected the vacant tables' glasses and plates. Drew stretched and touched Beverly's shoulder in order to formally signal the next transition.

"As lovely as this has been, we simply must bid adieu," she said as the hands on the wall clock drew towards midnight. "Tony and I may be brunching with his father in the early morning. And you know how I simply despise being fatigued during the day."

"Maybe at ten or so. We . . ."

"Have to be running along, I'm afraid," she finished and gave Tony a sharp elbow to the ribs. "You two should go for a late coffee sans Bledsloes. Isn't that right, my dearest?"

"Well, I guess we have to be running along then," her husband answered, erecting a relieved giggle from everyone.

"Call me tomorrow, Beverly," Drew concluded nicely and exited the table.

"Of course," Beverly said nonchalantly. The Bledsloes left the restaurant. Jack remained slightly uncomfortable without the wide safety net of Drew's presence as Beverly leaned on his shoulder.

"Coffee then," he said, composing himself.

"*Sans Bledsloes,*" Beverly giggled.

Jack took his date to his favorite coffee house on Cannery Row. They talked for an hour over their first cup. Their second cup was consumed late the next morning in Jack's kitchen.

CHAPTER 6

Drew stared at the toaster for a moment in their kitchen before pushing it away. The cord popped from the outlet it was attached to.

"TONY!" she bellowed.

"What?" her mate answered from across the linoleum. He pulled a beer from the giant refrigerator. Tony was hungover and irritable. Drew's voice only amplified the effect of both symptoms.

"Rosa didn't clean behind the appliances again. I have spoken to her repeatedly to *always* wipe behind the *appliances*! I can tell, you know. Just look at this dust gathered in the corner."

"So what? Nobody ever looks behind them, for Christ's sake!"

"That is simply *not* the point. The *point* is there are standards. I have my standards. You know that, Tony," she replied with a hand on her right hip, indicating that battling the logic would be a futile endeavor.

"Too well," he said gloomily. He took a long swig from the freshly opened lager. Drew shoved the toaster back into its substandard place and continued to stare at him.

"Well?"

"Well what, Drew?" he said. He felt himself already tugged over the line and rapidly sliding down into the mud.

"Are you going to speak with Rosa is *well what?* I simply will *not* live in a house where there is grime in every corner like some plumber's wife. Do I appear like a plumber's wife, Tony? Maybe I can buy a dirty apron and place curlers in my hair as well."

"No, Drew, you're just fantastic as is—really," he answered glumly.

"And exactly *what* are you implying with that comment, dear?"

"Nothing! Christ, I'll talk to her! Jesus, Drew, it's eight in the morning," he said, unbuttoning his shirt and escaping into the living room. She looked at him as he turned and disappeared around the corner. *He's gaining weight. Never even exercises anymore, at least not in the last five or six years. Pretty soon he's going to be fat. I'll be married to a fat businessman!* The thought revolted her. She went to the gym for spinning class with her girlfriends almost every morning, after their husbands left for the office. Some people cared about appearance and some did not.

Drew had met Anthony Bledsloe when she was a junior in college. It had been at an athletic club social at Yale, which invited certain members from its small, prestigious, sister college down the street. She had majored in general liberal arts, but her real incentive was the incentive of most upper society girls, who comprised her university. To find an affluent husband who could keep them in affluence. The weeding out process was relatively simple—most working class boys were at the various state colleges. Proximity was the key. If one wished to not associate with State, then one simply did not find oneself in their various and droll functions. And State did not mix with Yale, thus insuring that any young men in Ivy attendance would be genetically engineered from her pedigree.

And Anthony, at the time, seemed to be the likely finished product during Drew's informally extended debutante. It was reasoned that Tony would continue his football career after graduation. Drew marveled at the thought of being a professional athlete's wife. She would not only be the spouse of a millionaire but quite possibly appear on television. She envisioned herself on ladies' talk shows, revealing the pain and sacrifice of the lowly wife during the season—the nights alone as she supported her man on the field of battle, where he would return either with his shield or on it.

Tony's friends thought he would continue on this endeavor as well after throwing his cap to the wind. As a matter of fact, most everyone believed to see the name *Bledsloe* with a large number underneath glued to a bright jersey on Sunday afternoons. All felt quite certain, except one faction—the National Football League. Tony had been accepted for tryouts with the New England Patriots the summer following graduation. His fiancée, with a large rock on her finger, stood proudly by his side. She called her friends and family of the news and had already searched for houses in the area suitable for their status.

Then he was eliminated after the first cut.

Drew had revealed only to her best friend (which seemed to vary with the semester) that she considered calling the wedding off. She was still only twenty-two, from old money and good family name. And she was gorgeous. It was them, not her, who would come for the choosing. A different type of playing field but one she had grown well-accustomed to over her young years.

But, then there was the prospect that Tony would eventually own his father's company. She internally did not like Mr. Bledsloe Sr. Not at all, with his condescending harping of the infernal "ladder" he made his son climb. She believed that four years in the Ivy League sufficed a quick elevator to the upper floors. And the fact of his first year's salary of just over one hundred thousand dollars had infuriated her, although she kept quiet about the matter. This was Monterey, not Podunkville, like where Jack came from. A certain amount of class, seemingly ignorant to her husband's father, was expected from their society. As Tony stated, it was not Joe's Garage on the corner.

Drew Bledsloe had her standards, after all.

Tony's salary had doubled in the next five years and today brought in four hundred thousand with his profit sharing. Respectable, but not in Jack Strickland's league. And Drew wished very much to play in that league. Tony had refused her a new Jaguar she wanted. And he complained incessantly over her credit cards. She didn't want a limit like some schoolgirl on an allowance. If he graduated to his father's position, he would double his income again and possibly not feel the constant urge to harass her so. *If* his bothersome father would simply retire as his age deemed proper, she reasoned. *If* her husband would simply stand up to him. But neither Bledsloe had accommodated her as of yet.

And now Junior was getting fat.

She pulled out the small wine rack on the kitchen counter. *A glass of Merlot would be nice,* she thought, noticing the not wiped area behind the bottles. A corkscrew was retrieved and driven deep. With several twisting motions, accompanied by a small grimace on her face, a stifled selection from Napa was finally allowed to breathe. She knew that to enjoy a glass properly, the breathing should be allowed at room temperature for approximately three hours but forewent the procedure and filled a large glass almost to the brim, which was also not protocol. Indifferent as she was, outside the sight of her peers, she followed Tony to the living room.

"So . . . Beverly and Jack seem to be a match. Wonder where they went?" she said slyly.

"Probably his bedroom." Tony took another large draw from his beer. He stared listlessly at a tennis match on the television.

"Anthony!" she exclaimed with dramatic effect to the remark. "I can assure you that my friend is *not* of the caliber who would simply jump into bed on a first date. Even with one Mr. Jack Strickland!" Tony looked away from the match he wasn't really watching and began to laugh.

"What's so funny?"

"You are," he replied. He turned his head back to the screen and began flipping channels.

"Oh, I am now, am I?"

"Not the type my ass. With his money? Please, Drew, who do you think you're talking to?"

"Not to mention that I do *not* favor the implication towards one of my dearest friends," she added.

"Heaven forbid that we offend the clique. Christ, she was practically pile-driving him at the restaurant last night. I'm sure Beverly would be just as fascinated with Jack if he was an electrician—even though he kind of acts like one sometimes."

Drew sat quietly, forgetting for the moment her defense of Beverly's damaged reputation. "He does have that demeanor of . . . the lower background, I'm afraid. He and that lummox Sarge are two peas in a pod, it seems."

"That's because he was enlisted once as well—navy, remember?" Tony said.

"That is exactly my point. Too much of that . . . *element* in our Jack Strickland. Hopefully Beverly can smooth him out a bit. It isn't impossible to teach one from that environment how to conduct oneself when one reaches *ours,* is it, dear?"

"I don't know, Drew. He's on the rough side, I suppose, but I like him. Like I said—talks like a regular guy. Reminds me of some of my teammates at Yale. Come from money but still know how to take a hit."

"Please, dear, you know how I simply detest bringing up those days of dirty lockers and tackle dummies. And I am not saying that I *dislike* Jack. As I stated perfectly clear, I believe he just isn't of our . . . class. He doesn't dress well, for instance. Which may be forgivable if he were simply *aware* of the fact. But he is oblivious and apathetic to it. If one is to reside here, one simply must dress accordingly or else one might be mistaken for a tourist. And I do not enjoy sitting next to tourists, dear. And he is not the *least* bit interested in social enhancement. He has a duty to social enhancement with the wealth he has achieved, Tony. Why, I brought the matter up last week, and he practically *dismissed* me!"

"Christ, Drew, you asked him for money?"

"I requested his *support,* Tony. Others in the community with much less means have contributed greatly to the organization."

"If he doesn't want to give away his money, then that's his business, Drew."

"That's *just* like you! My own husband cannot even be supportive to a pertinent cause. Too busy running around your father's office, I suppose." Tony slammed his beer down on the end table. A foam rose, spilling on the wood.

"*First* of all, it's *my* office! And once Pop retires, it's going to be *my* company! You see, Drew, I have a *job*! I have other things to worry about, probably like Jack does, other than your goddamn high society social crusade!"

"I have a job, Tony!" she shouted.

"Drew, you never had a job your entire life, short of selling lemonade on your dad's porch. You're a volunteer. You don't bring a goddamn penny into this house. Your *job* is tea parties and martinis, where you sit with your other snobs, talking about a bunch of fags who for whatever reason feel they're jaded because they play on the other side of the field. And all of that would be fine except you and your unemployed cronies, also living high on the hog off their husbands, run around shooting your mouths off at people like Strickland and Miles and anyone else in your path, how they should be as keyed up as you are about something that is fucking *stupid* anyway!" Tony had risen, and they stood in the familiar glare of each other.

"Well, at least Jack doesn't have to run to his daddy every time he wants a day off, now does he? Jack is independent, isn't he, dear? He made something of himself!"

"*I* made something of myself," Tony said in a low tone with a menacing step, which caused a tremor of fear in his wife. "I make close to a half-million dollars a year. Almost a *half-million*! Only a spoiled bitch wouldn't appreciate that figure."

"Oh, so *I'm* the bitch, am I? Marvelous! Simply astounding, coming from a has-been field player!" Tony stopped short as if slapped. He opened and closed his mouth several times, and then turned away and slouched back into the couch.

"So, that's it," he said, softly gazing at the wall behind the television. He chuckled as if he suddenly realized the humor, long after the others had quit laughing. "Of course. Why didn't I see it? You still resent you aren't the N.F.L. wife. Well, you know what, Drew? I tried. Most guys never even play high school ball. I *started* my sophomore year in college. And I got cut in the pros. So what? At least I did something. And, I still make four hundred thousand greenbacks a year, Pop's company or not. Look at you. Nothing but a leech with a halfway decent rack. In ten years, you won't even be worth the price of one of Sarge's mixers." He stood again, reaching for his coat and stepped toward the door, almost brushing roughly into his wife.

"And just where do you think you're going?"

"Out," he said. "I don't want to even look at you, Drew. You make me sick." She began to rebut, but Tony had already shut the door behind him.

◆ ◆ ◆

"Donja ever get married, Miles," Tony slurred. "Fuckin' for the bluuuujays, thas what married is. Fuckin' bunch of leech *cunts*," he added in a boisterous voice, causing many heads to turn abruptly from the lounge. Sarge gave a warning look to both of them across the bar.

"Easy, Tony. Keep the voice down, will ya? People are staring." Tony had skipped brunch and gone directly to Bully's from his house and was on his seventh or tenth pint of lager.

"Fuckin' cunts," he said more softly. "Donja do it, Miles. Never."

"I already did it, remember, pal? Twice. Both got the alimony before finally replacing me. I'm with you, big guy, just not so loud, ok?"

"Fuckin' alimony. Can't escape it, old boy. Bitch gets haf if I dump her and mor'n haf if I stay. Less she's cheatin.' Hey, Miles, old boy, y'wanna fuck Drew? She'd do it, y'know. Jus' gotta hav' a paycheck an' sign over, old boy." He began to laugh hysterically.

"Not funny, Tony."

"Oh yeah. Lotta funny stuff in Monterey. All the leeches liv' in The Bay, yessir, old boy. To the leeches!" he announced, raising his glass to Sarge, who shook his head slowly.

"Getting a little loud, Mr. Bledsloe," the bartender warned sternly.

"Oops! Sorry ol' Sarge," Tony said, saluting. "Hey, I gotta idea here. Gotta good idea. Drew can marry ol' Sarge. H'can have her. See how she likes ol' Sarge. Hey, Sarge! Y'make four hunnerad a year?"

"No," Sarge said, looking at Miles.

"C'mon, Tony," Miles said. He lifted a hand of peace to the bartender.

"Nope, dinit think so. Ne'er mind, Sarge, you don't have the waddayacallit, you sojer boys. Don't got the right pay grade. Yeah, thas it, old boy, sorry. Don't feel so bad, Sarge. I don't got the right pay grade either. Hey, Miles. Where's Jack's number? Gotta call the old boy. Jack's got the pay grade alright. Gotta call Jack."

"We should go, Tony," Miles said, tugging at his sleeve and grabbing his coat.

"How 'bout you?" Tony leered at the waitress. "I'm in your pay grade, aren't I?" She only smiled and looked at Sarge, who was not smiling at all. "Yep, one night in the ol' Marriot, sweetheart. Howsa that grade, honey?" Sarge made a motion to Miles.

"Let's go, Tony," Miles said, helping him up. "We'll put some down at my place and watch DVDs, ok? Forget all this stuff. C'mon, pal."

"Yep, forget all this stuff," he answered, staggering to the door. "N'more pay grades." It was only 2:30 p.m. as Miles partly walked and mostly carried Tony to the car. At Miles' house, more tin soldiers died between them and Tony eventually passed out on his friend's couch late at night, still muttering about Drew and pay grades.

CHAPTER 7

July

Jack woke up slightly past 7:00 a.m. to the usual distant crash of the waves near his cove. He listened to the rhythm for a few minutes before dropping his legs over the large mahogany king bed. He had only been asleep for a few hours, yet felt fully rejuvenated, not even noticing the effects of the many drinks the prior evening. The woman next to him stirred and mumbled something incoherently. He eased himself slowly to the floor, careful not to wake her, partly from consideration but mostly because of his revel in the morning's solitude. He walked barefoot and in boxers to the kitchen, put on a full pot of coffee and looked out the front window to The Bay as the pot gurgled and dripped.

Beverly had more or less moved in since their first meeting over a month ago, almost without Jack even realizing the novel modification. The first night had led to multiple nights, in which Jack had suddenly found himself in a declared relationship. Three weeks after being set up by Drew, Beverly had stated that she loved him. As he sensed himself trapped in a socialized corner, he made the commonest of errors to his gender.

He said it back.

Which was not to say that he didn't really like her and couldn't have loved her eventually if given enough time. But he realized, well after the fact, that his response was more a concoction of Sarge's Rummers while on another couples' binge with the Bledsloes, which had enhanced his speedy reply late on that particular night. And he could not take it back or even have the remark reviewed for nullification, due to extenuating circumstances of the vast amount of rum, which swished around in his head at the time. Women are allowed the usage of the phrase in haste, in which men are required careful forethought well in advance. And Jack, like most when the initial remark is uttered, was not given time for consideration of the subject.

And, she began to bring things over, once he verbally leapt off. First, a hair dryer and other minor female paraphernalia. Then a few sets of clothes followed by a couple DVDs. Then she had even decorated a few things "to brighten up the house." Which wasn't to say not completely nice, although did give Jack the distant warning signal of intrusion. And the indication proved correct on his internal radar. Half of his bedroom closet was now full of her stuff. And he had the vague discomfort that in another month or two, hints of matrimony would be warming up on deck. It was just so . . . .

Fast.

He could not help remembering Everett's advice earlier in the summer, when he had just been indoctrinated into the Bledsloe cult. It could be that he and Beverly were indeed one of those super-accelerated-love-at-first-sight events, which everyone knows about but no one can place exactly. However, those same seers can always call to mind several instances where the event was rained out completely before the end of the third inning. And Jack feared the storm clouds he saw on the horizon, the far off thunder of Everett's voice in warning. And maybe he should heed this bit of advisement. He still did not realize his own wealth. Even with the large house right on The Bay. Same watery jewel he strolled around, fresh out of high school, without the recent worries that he possessed today. At eighteen, he was quite aware of his status. Even with more hair and less lines in his cheeks.

His social standing nagged at the inner gray matter the longer he stayed as a local. Not a complex query really. The millionaire question of *what if he wasn't one?* Would Drew and Tony be so overly chummy with him? Would Beverly? There were certain specifics. Variables, if one will. Variable "A" was that Beverly looked like a supermodel. Variable "B" was that he was relatively decent looking. And when a woman like that was present, he was also aware, like most ordinary men are subconsciously aware, there exists a certain invisible velvet rope, where the social doormen enforce strict rules protecting access to that type of woman. And that specific entrance required a huge cover charge. The engineer's mind went to work on the equation. Ordinary Jack versus Multimillionaire Jack. Ordinary Jack walks down the street and Beverly passes the other way. Or even Ordinary Jack encounters her at the lounge. A simple equation. Ordinary Jack + Beverly = Instant Adoration. And somehow the result didn't quite match the answer in the back of the book. And the distant muffled voice of Young Jack nodded congruently.

But that was a long time ago, when one Seaman Recruit Strickland had been snubbed at the local pub by the native girl. For a simple dance. Jack still remembered, not the refusal, but the *dismissal*. The stare and eyes behind it demanding contrition for his audacity. The glower, which clearly stated that one residing on top of The Hill in no way made one a resident, and please return to your quarters without further disturbance. He wondered what that girl was doing today and with whom she was doing it? Did she graduate and marry a Bledsloe as well? Did the privileged ever grow out of their pretentiousness? Or was the tradition so ingrained that conceit became customary? What would Young Drew have said if Young Jack asked her to dance at that pub many years ago? The Bledsloes and Miles never acted in such a manner around him. But he certainly sensed their perception of hierarchy towards Sarge. A sense of tone, abruptly changed when direction of converse shifted from Sarge to him, like an unknown riptide circling just below the calm water above.

That's because you're one of them now.

Actually, he was not one of them. He was richer than all of them put together, if truth be told, and his mind indeed searched for social accuracy. His consulting with the San Francisco based company kept him just busy enough not to drown in a pool of bored tears, but he could retire from all of it if he wished. He could spend every night at Bully's with the Bledsloes and Beverly and every late morning walking off an aching head on the shoreline. Nap the afternoon away and rinse and repeat cycle on high. There were worse methods to spend your allotted days in the bank.

But the little voice still troubled him. Everett was married to the same woman he started with, before the invention transformed both of their lives. And he still ran the farm while calling Jack occasionally with designs of their next endeavor. Everett still wanted to be an engineer. His mental outlet wasn't located at Bully's, shorted out by the gold pirates' grog. Everett had formed in *his* mind their next great success. All Jack had accomplished in the last few months was getting moderately drunk every night. And the voice called him on his recent escapades. It put out the warning pitch that the new gal was pushing too fast. Keeping his brain on hold with fantastic sex so he wouldn't think too much. Like the old adage of the camel slowly pushing itself into the tent, against the owner's wishes. But, the sex was fantastic. The little voice was muffled most nights. Only in the solitude of morning was when it screamed.

"Jackers!" He snapped out of his reverie and spilled a third of the coffee on his fingertips. *Jackers* had developed into her pet name for him. She found the new endearment amusing. Inwardly, he did not.

"Geez, Beverly, I thought you were still asleep," he said, shaking his hand into the sink.

"Well, I *was* asleep. And now I am not," she replied. She took his arm and kissed the first two knuckles. "Poor little hand. Are you alright?"

"Yeah, fine. You just startled me."

"Good," she said, letting go. "You have to get dressed. We're meeting Drew and Tony at the wine expo at ten-thirty. Sharp."

"Is that today? I'm really not into those things, Bev."

"Yes, that *is* today. Drew's organizational committee will be there too. Oh, Jackers, cheer up and I'll guide you properly into buying us some Sonoma Merlot. Besides, Drew needs the support."

"I think the last thing Drew is in need of is support."

"Why are you so opposed to her cause, Jack?" The pet name dropped off the edge with a hint of irritability. "She's just trying to improve matters in her corner of the world. Is that so intolerable?"

"I'm not opposed to her doing it, but c'mon, Bev . . . look at her 'cause.' Illegal alien discrimination. Gay discrimination. And what's her latest—oh, that's right, a memorial to all lesbians killed in foreign wars. Like there isn't already a memorial for everyone lost overseas. Why can't she take a normal course, like feed the homeless or something?"

She narrowed her eyes slightly. "It wouldn't hurt you to donate, you know . . . I mean, with all that money. You wouldn't even miss it."

"That's not the point, Beverly. If I want to donate, I'll give to a cancer research center. Or UNICEF. But that stuff? I just don't care about it. I don't know why *she* cares about it. Gays in the military, for instance. She's never even *been* in the military. And she's not gay. Illegal aliens? She's an American citizen, for God's sake."

"Well, opinions are like . . . well, you know, Jack," she replied, walking off toward the shower room.

Jesus, was that a fight? I think we just had our first fight. Not a smack down but definitely a few stiff jabs thrown. All because Drew's her best friend and she's pissed. Like I'm obligated to support every asinine project her friend comes up with in-between champagne brunches and Sarge's Rummers. Beverly will probably be steamed all day now. And tell Drew what I said the first second out of my sight. Who cares? Her friend's projects are asinine and anyone outside of the city district would think so too.

But she emerged forty minutes later as if the matter had not occurred at all and later took Jack's arm as they went out the door. And he soon forgot all about it. But Beverly did not. However, she kept her anger well-concealed. It was her training, like Drew's, that taught her the art of camouflage to what could be detrimental, only revealing the true self when it was too late for the other. The little voice in Jack's head did not forget as well. The argument had awakened and stirred it out of bed, and it was already scribing the notes, recording the whole event to be organized and presented to the Conscious at the prudent time.

During the summer months, Monterey cashed in its chips. From late May to early September, the weekends transitioned into grand events and spectacular expositions, carefully orchestrated by the city council and attracted all of the genres. There were jazz festivals. There were blues festivals. Classic automobile expos. Corvette and crotch rocket conventions. All packing the city's two to three hundred dollar a night motels, hotels and bed and breakfasts. Filling The Wharf and Row's restaurants and touristy gift shops. Every day until Fall's cold hands retrieved the tourists and cast them back to the plains of mediocrity. Once cleared, The Bay would breathe a sigh of relief en route to the bank deposits.

Jack remembered the same during his days at the Language Institute on The Hill. Only then he was more apt to avoid the crowds, whereas now he was thrown directly in their midst. During the summer, Drew's organization campaigned vigorously with literature, buttons and bumper stickers and insured every visitor from around the globe was well aware of the level of inequality, which they somehow didn't notice in their everyday lives. And today was no different at the wine festival, where Beverly dragged a reluctant Jack by the fingertips to Drew's information stand. Tony was there, leaning on a back table, slaying a lager and appearing as strained as Jack felt. Drew stopped mid-sentence to a woman who held one of her pamphlets and rushed over and gave Beverly a hug that signified separation of years instead of mere hours.

"And my dear Jack," she exclaimed. She grabbed both of his cheeks with her thumbs and index fingers.

"Hi, Drew."

"*Hi Drew*," she mimicked. "Don't look so humdrum, Jack, although I am certain that your excitement equally matches my husband's."

"I never said I didn't want to come," Tony replied from the background with a tone that indicated he needn't have said anything at all.

"Of course you didn't, dear. But now that I have my best friend upon arrival, you boys can run off and play for a bit. You have my permission."

Tony popped off the table. "What do you say, Jack?" he said, finishing the bottle with one gulp.

"I could walk around, I guess."

Her husband sprang around the stand and slapped Jack on the back. "We'll be back later. Don't wait on us for lunch, though."

"Why would we?" Drew replied icily. The two men ambled around, eyeing the different companies' wine stands under the pretense of interest.

"So why is Drew's association here? Isn't this a wine thing?" Jack asked.

"Drew's *association* is pretty much anywhere and everywhere it wants to be. All she has to do for permit is call Miles."

"I see." They walked around slowly for a few more minutes.

"To tell the truth, I hate this kind of shit," Tony said, well out of eyesight of the women.

"Me too," Jack laughed. "But swear to secrecy, or it will get back to Beverly."

"Blood oath. So what do you say—Bully's?" Tony suggested with a wry grin.

"There's an idea. We'll see how Sarge is doing." They made way through the congested town, crossing over Del Monte Street and passed The Wharf, to the ten minute walk toward Cannery Row. Bully's was quiet this midday as the crowds were at the festival and would hold until sunset before invading The Row, where they would speak with new found knowledge of sudden connoisseurs. The bartender stood idly and talked with the waitress who looked equally bored. He gave a wave to Jack's direction, and then eyed Tony.

"Mr. Bledsloe," he said evenly.

"Sarge! So, how's the soldier of fortune business treating you today?"

"Just fine, Mr. Bledsloe. Rummers?"

"Gentleman and a scholar. Bring us a pitcher. Hey, Jack, I'll be right back." Tony darted off toward the jukebox. He spent a considerable amount of time browsing the tracks until Bobbi, the server, found her way over to help him. They spoke in hushed tones as Tony's fingers traced the selection buttons back and forth.

"So how are you holding, Sarge? Another weekend at the grindstone?" Jack said.

"No different than any other weekend, I guess. For about two more months anyway until we graduate," the bartender answered. He twisted a clean towel around the inside of a freshly washed pint mug.

"Know where you're going yet?"

"Nope, figure they'll let me know at the last minute, like usual."

"Yeah," Jack laughed. "Some things never change. And what will my entourage do when you're gone? Who's going to mix the Rummers, Sarge?"

"I'm sure they'll be fine," he answered and gave an icy look to Tony and Bobbi, still at the box. Jack sat silent for a few seconds.

"What's up, Sarge?"

"Nothing. None of my business." He put the glass on the shelf and dipped another into the soapy water sink under the bar table. Jack looked over at the two. Bobbi was obviously perturbed as the voices fell even lower.

"You're kidding?" Jack said, lowering his tone as well.

"Like I said, none of my business," Sarge replied, stiffly topping off his drink from the pitcher, which sat beside him. Jack sat back and drew it to his lips.

"Tell me, Sarge, what do you really think of the locals? Really?"

"Better not to say."

"C'mon. One military guy to another." The bartender put his cloth down on the counter and slowly wiped an area that was already clean.

"Truth?"

"Yeah, truth," Jack said.

"I guess it doesn't matter since I'll be putting in notice in a month. Not like I need a reference. I think they are all a horse's ass, Jack. I think they are a bunch of spoiled snots who never grew out of daddy's wallet. Especially his wife." He jerked a thumb towards Tony. "A little rich golly-gee-do-gooder who's never done anything in her life. I almost feel sorry for him. Almost. That enough truth for you, Jack?"

"Christ. And me?"

"I think you're getting sucked right into it. Take no offense since I know you were up The Hill—once upon a time. And that was a long time ago. But take that girl of yours, and maybe I'm out of line, but if you can't trust the only sober person in the bar, then who can you trust? I listen to her and Drew talk. I listen when they don't know I'm listening. They don't know it because I don't exist to them. I know what they think, Jack. They look at me like they'd look at a piece of gum they just stepped on in the road. But it's not politically correct for them to say it out loud, now is it? So they cover it nicely, which is even worse than just saying it. You should hear what they say when they think Bobbi and I aren't eavesdropping."

"So what do they say, Sarge?"

"You're a meal ticket, Jack. And I'm sorry as hell to have to be the one to tell you. If Tony was any kind of friend, he would have already. Don't be too pissed. Every native girl here is looking for one. So they can go and play like Drew. A life of leisure. That's why Drew set you up. You're an ok looking guy, but let's get a little bit of reality here. You think that gorgeous looking girlfriend of yours would have jumped feet over hands if you weren't rich? And she's what—late twenties? She knows the clock to the expiration date of that particular ticket. And I'm going to tell you something else and you can take heed or go and be pissed off some more. But consider it a solid. From as you say, one enlisted guy to one ex-enlisted who made good. And I don't want to see you get punked because of these assholes. And they are assholes, Jack. About nine months ago she was with another guy—also pretty well off. Not like you but enough to keep her in the mid-morning aerobics class and cafes in the afternoon if they married. Guy had city connections and funds therewith. Type of funds that bought votes, if you know what I mean. Same routine. Drew set them up and a few months later she moved in."

"What happened?" Jack asked softly.

"Problem with women is they have the ability to conceal themselves only so much. I had been working here part-time for only a little while. She and Drew used to come in and bitch about him. How he wouldn't tie the two and a half-hitch. They had only been together something like four or five months. She finally talked him into a joint bank account as a token of faith. So he does that. And she starts spending like one of you navy guys on shore leave. She almost quit her job too. Thought she had him. Luckily, the guy had already been around the block and up and down the side streets a few times. And that past stroll resulted in two costly divorces for him."

"Christ, Sarge, this is Beverly you're talking about?"

"Yep. And he broke it off. Told her he wouldn't even consider marriage for at least five years. So she called his bluff. The ultimatum of a timeline. Attached with an 'or else.' He picked the *else*. She moved out a week later."

Jack sat quietly for a moment as his synapses reworked the equation. "Sounds like a smart guy."

"Yeah, he *was* smart, Jack. He was and Tony wasn't. But you already know about that. You also know Beverly's ex."

"I *know* this guy?"

"Miles. Oh, no one mentioned that to you, did they? Too awkward in their circle jerk, I guess. Bet a two-dollar bill your girl never even hinted at it either."

"No, she didn't. Neither did Tony or Drew. I'll be goddamned."

"Sound like real pals. Be careful, Jack," Sarge finished as Tony came back over. An old Journey song began to fill the lounge.

"Music for the soul, right, old boy?" Tony said, nudging Jack in the ribs harder than he would have liked. His eyes darted nervously back and forth from Jack to Sarge, to the array of bottles stacked on the shelf. "Say, Jack, let's grab a table in the lounge so we don't resemble a couple of barflies."

"Yeah, ok. Good talking to you, Sarge . . . and thanks," Jack said. Sarge nodded and went back to cleaning the glasses and mugs.

"What was all that about?" Tony asked, on the other side of the pub. "You guys look like you just broke Watergate or something."

"Nothing, Tony. Just two military guys shooting the shit," Jack replied.

"Oh," he answered uncomfortably, rubbing his finger on the droplets outside the glass.

"So how are you and Drew getting on these days?"

"Oh, you know. Drew is Drew. She's been getting pissy because I've been so busy lately. Goddamn feds are doing an audit on the company."

"Really? Shit, Tony."

"Oh no, nothing to worry about, old boy. Just routine. They do that from time to time to justify themselves. Keeps the untouchables happy and all. But Drew doesn't get it—that sometimes you have to buck up a little and light the midnight oil. In a way, I'm glad she has that damn organization of hers to keep at least halfway occupied or she'd be up my ass twenty-four-seven, you know? Speaking of, you and Beverly seem to be moving along," he said. He shifted his eyes to the other end of the lounge.

"We're doing alright, I guess."

"Careful, buddy, soon she'll make an honest man of you."

"We'll see, Tony." They drank the afternoon away, forgetting much about the festivities downtown. Jack had found that his tolerance for the Rummer had greatly increased since his arrival in May. At 5:00 p.m., as the event closed, people began to return to The Wharf and Row. Drew and Beverly came with them and not at all pleased.

"Well," Drew said as she sat down at the table. "You boys seemed to have had no trouble entertaining yourselves."

"Sarge's fault," Tony answered comically as Jack stifled a guffaw with his hand to an equally annoyed Beverly. "He'll vouch for it. We tried to stop him but he just kept making new pitchers. RIGHT SAAAARGE?" he called to him who only raised a hand in resignation.

"Oh for Heaven's sake, please keep your voice down, will you? It seems us girls have a bit of catching up to do indeed. Yooohooo!" she catcalled, raising her hand to the waitress. Bobbi came over and glanced at everyone except Tony, who kept his eyes on the table. "Yes, dear, we'll have another pitcher, please, with two glasses for ourselves as our gentlemen seemed to have neglected us for the day. And I would like a small orange slice in mine. Last time I didn't get my slice."

"You bet," she said curtly and walked off.

"Do I detect an *attitude* in her today? I simply cannot tolerate when someone in service has an attitude. As if it is a grand chore to simply do her job."

"She doesn't have an attitude, Drew," Tony said.

"No, dear," his wife answered slowly. "I'm certain I am *quite* mistaken."

"So how did the stand go?" Jack interrupted, altering the subject quickly.

"Oh, my dear Jack, you do not have to pretend at this point to be interested. But if you *must* know, I found several more major supporters, even among the boorish visitors here to our lovely town. One from Nevada who owns a chain of casinos. A dear Native American man. So tragic, what we have done to those poor souls. I simply wanted to apologize right then and there."

"Oh right, I'm sure he's devastated by his string of slot machines. Probably suffering unbearably. Hey, I know, maybe you could offer his teepee back," Tony said.

"Such sarcasm, dear, I . . ." Drew began and was interrupted by the returning server.

"Here we go," she said, plopping the pitcher down. A run of red mix dripped on the sides. "And two glasses, one orange slice."

"This is a large slice. I do remember asking for a small one."

"Jesus, Drew, just cut it in half," Tony said. He met Bobbi's eyes briefly.

"Of course. I shall cut it in half. No, dear, don't trouble yourself." She took the fruit out and neatly divided it, tossing one half in her glass and the other on the server's drink tray. "There. All fixed, dear."

"Anything else?" Bobbi asked.

"Well, actually . . ." Drew began.

"No. Not for now," Tony said, cutting her off. The waitress left the table toward the bar where she and Sarge began to speak in quiet tones. Drew lightly twirled the orange in the drink with the plastic stir as the others sat in uncomfortable silence.

"As if it is my fault she's a bar maid," Drew said. "Maybe with a little ambition, she wouldn't have to concern herself with orange slices. I often wonder what sort of man is attracted toward women of such mediocrity. What are your thoughts, my dear Jack? Are you attracted to women without aspirations?"

"I don't know her, Drew," he answered quietly, avoiding Beverly's eyes.

"Ah, you misunderstand me, of course," Drew continued. "It is not the person but the *type*. They are always the same, I'm afraid. Searching for someone who will rescue them of their daily drudgery. How fortunate you have my best friend to save you from them. You do feel fortunate, don't you, Jack?"

"He feels fortunate alright," Beverly said, stroking his shoulder. "Even if he did abandon me all afternoon."

"Guilty," Jack confessed. "Sorry, I can only look at wine and cheese for so long."

"You can make it up by taking me to Cello's. They have excellent Tiramisu. What do you think, Drew? Should they escort us to an expensive dinner as penance?" Beverly chided.

"Oh, but that would be a magnificent start," she answered jovially but stared hard at her husband's eyes, which seemed glued to his Rummer.

They finished the pitcher, and Drew insisted on a cab back to the downtown area, claiming to have already been on her feet all day (actually it was only a quarter of it). Jack noticed that his head was only reeling mildly as he had paced himself through the drinks most of the afternoon. Tony had not and seemingly gulped one Rummer down after another as if in a sprint to the inebriated finish line, before his wife came down from the stands. He had been quiet most of the day and evening, becoming more so through the pasta dinner and several bottles of Merlot. Jack's tab had again come to a few hundred dollars. He didn't concern himself much as the Bledsloes parted ways and he and Beverly walked home. *Maybe Sarge was wrong,* he thought, looking at her shapely figure, knowing what was to come later.

Maybe this was the exception to the rule.

CHAPTER 8

August

Jack tapped his fingers nervously as he listened to the dial ring across the country. Everett's slight drawl, with a chorus of children's muffled voices in the background, came on and wished all well and stated to leave a message of whatever urgent matter was at hand. Jack put the phone down and paced around the living room wondering why he was so antsy. *Nothing to do with your drinking every night, I'm sure,* his own answering service ringed in his head when signaled upon for explanation of his recent jitters. *Keep this pace and soon you'll be a candidate for Celebrity Rehab—Monterey.*

And it was true. Prior to his arrival, his consumption was strictly on a light social level. A rarity during the week. Now it was a rarity not to indulge. His first stop in May at Bully's had metamorphosed into a nightly and sometimes daily habit with the Bledsloes and usually Miles. Added lately, Beverly was there most nights after the gift shop she managed closed. In fact, Beverly was pretty much everywhere Jack was all of the time now. She had more than once dropped the hint of the erroneous necessity of paying rent when she spent all of her time in Jack's house anyway. These subtle insinuations only reminded him of Sarge's prediction weeks ago.

He had gone to San Francisco again last week for his quarterly meeting with the professional suits and strangely found that he relished being absent from Monterey. Everett had passed on this meeting seeing it as a waste of time. A peace in the hotel room, which was deficient in his own household as Beverly became more agitated by the week from Jack's delay of her domestic relocation. And they began to bicker about other things as well. Jack had evolved in his adult life to a staunch conservative, this position largely acquired by earning a college degree in youth by his own hand. So he naturally assumed his ideology was shared by everyone else as well as people do when the circumstances of outside forces construct and mold belief systems. He drank his lifeblood from the bowl of self-reliance. When he had nowhere to go at eighteen, he had enlisted into the service and used the service to put him through school. It never occurred to him to apply for welfare, therefore he failed to appreciate the occurrence in others. And Beverly, who sipped from not only an opposite bowl, but an entirely separate and exclusive restaurant, had bloomed into an ultra-utopian, whose views were in direct opposition to what Jack considered basic common sense.

The root of one conflict was over a future child, yet to be conceived. Jack was uncertain how the argument began, not realizing that in the dating process the parties involved are in constant state of sending reconnaissance scouts from the subconscious on missions for intelligence, prior to committing the full assault of marriage. Jack had insisted in the discourse that the child, whether boy or girl, would be trained in self-defense as a precaution to the contentions that periodically emerge in the human genre. He in school had taken up wrestling for sport and found its use in other purposes as the situation dictated. Simply put, it kept him from a thorough ass-kicking more than once in the extended turmoil known as adolescence. Beverly, in turn, held the standpoint that violence was never the answer and lectured Jack adamantly on his rustic lack of civility, contending that the ideal future contained a world where all conflicts would be resolved through reasonable and rational discourse.

"Problem with that wonderful theory, Bev, is that the entire history of the planet disagrees with you. Ask the Jews sometime," Jack had stated. And like every conceived personage who doesn't have a reasonable counterargument, she drowned him out by talking louder and faster, believing a high volume of repetition somehow conceded her point. A point, which Jack found in the real life world quite ludicrous.

And although the hotly angered debate may have been laughed at later as the subject was, after all, over an imaginary child, it held in Jack's mind that the topic may pertain to a very real child if matters continued to advance at the rate Beverly wished them to progress. And that Beverly would wish this child to be fed from the chinaware located across the street. Jack believed in the theory of opposite attraction only when applied to the formations of atoms, not couples. Which meant a lifetime of heated arguments, derived from similar elements from the above. Also that she waited for this transformation of hypothetical children to real ones, gauged from her biological Timex. And she would only wait for so long.

Which is the snare? he thought. A simple but unstated truth was most men would greatly prefer to avoid marriage altogether if they were not afraid. Afraid of losing what they have. Fear of losing that steady piece, if a greater truth be revealed. And the difference between the two sexes is that women were born, misfortunately, with a timeline and men were not. The timeline, which pushed men into marriage a great deal more quickly than they would have been shoved otherwise. Jack believed most men, left to their own devices, wouldn't marry until well into their forties. But they got sucked in, he reasoned. To take the plunge when they don't really fancy swimming at the moment. The women first press for engagement, nag at it and in the end threaten for it. The end of the piece. And the male believes himself intelligent for the bought time purchased for the reprieve. But then the furlough slips by, and he is shackled and led away for good, the cost of his escape—half of his salary.

And Jack did not feel like swimming or even dipping his toe in the water just yet. He didn't even want to put on his trunks. And the topic of the depths recurred more and more frequently. Very soon it would be the only topic. And he and Beverly were opposite particles. In beliefs and ideology. In core of being. Destined to repel each other through the rotations of life or at least push to the outskirts of the institution. Very much like . . . .

Tony and Drew.

Which made sense as Beverly was Drew's best friend. And he was fully aware that Drew's mouth had Bev's ear. Drew's other half had taken the swan dive before he was even old enough to know to bring a pair of floats along. And although they were perceived as animated, it seemed to Jack that Tony was drowning for his efforts. He could confirm that Tony and Bobbi, the waitress, were a regular item. Probably had been for some time now. And he was pretty certain that Drew was at least suspicious at best and casually indifferent at worst. Who knew? Maybe she had someone as well. Maybe they both knew, and it was less trouble and expensive to keep quiet about it as long as the money kept rolling in. Maybe that was how things were done with the natives of Monterey. And maybe, if Jack didn't slow down a bit, it was quite possible that he would fly off the cliff and into the ocean and join his companion, Mr. Bledsloe.

Jack walked down to his coffee shop, several blocks from Bully's. It had become another safe haven, like his cove and sat across from The Aquarium. Old lounge chairs filled the room as the pastries and beverages were simply laid out on the counter. Open trash cans stood in the corners for the refuse. None of his clique would bother him here, opting for the more chic cafe down the street. As he sat down, his cell phone chimed from his jacket pocket. Fumbling to open it, he saw *Everett* flashing urgently on the small screen.

"Finally," he answered.

"So, what's the emergency? You left three messages in two hours. The Bay didn't evaporate, did it?" Everett joshed.

"Still here, but a mist is covering it today," Jack answered casually as people do when the small talk is about to cross the bridge to larger fields.

"What's wrong, Jack?" Everett asked seriously. He felt the tug line of strain at the other end of the country. Jack began slowly at first, Everett interrupting only occasionally to ask questions here and there but grew more silent as his friend unloaded the past few months, up to the possibility of him being relieved from bachelorhood in the near future.

"How long have you known this gal?" Everett asked.

"I don't know—two, two and a half months, tops. Drew set us up."

"She's Drew's friend?"

"Best friend, actually," Jack replied.

"Hmmm . . . if they really have those. And she's already living with you?"

"More or less, Everett."

"Well, what is it? More or less?"

"More. Actually she wants it to be official and cancel her lease."

"Uh huh," Everett said. Jack allowed the silence as his friend double-checked the equation's product. "And I bet she's talking about the long walk down the short aisle."

"Pretty much every other day."

"All in two months . . . more or less," Everett said.

"That's about the scope of it," Jack concluded.

"Well, buddy, it doesn't sound like a relationship. Sounds like an *agenda*. And not a hard one to figure—on my end anyway. You want to know what I think?"

"That's why I called you, Everett," Jack said impatiently.

"Ok, here she goes. You're a millionaire. She sees her pal, Drew, living the life while not having to work at all. She wants the same."

"That's what my buddy the bartender said."

"Sounds like a smart fellow," Everett replied.

"Yeah, he is. And apparently she was shacked up with another social climber not too long ago. I know him. He's not rich but probably pretty well off."

"Jack, there's your kewpie doll wrapped up nice. Not just an agenda, but a pattern to go with it."

"Hell, Everett, you got married after six months," Jack said.

"I wasn't wealthy at the time, Jack. I was a struggling student, trying to run a more struggling farm. Sorry, but a little easier to be objective on my end."

"True," Jack conceded. "Hey, Everett, why don't you take me up on that vacation down here. Stay at my place. I'll take you around and let you see for yourself. Plus you get my obscene view of The Bay from the living room window."

"I don't know . . . . I'm not real read up on high society," Everett hesitated.

"Forget high society. We'll get a couple of mid-society drafts, and you can get a firsthand look at my entourage."

"I guess Floyd could run the place for a week without setting the fields on fire. And Shirley keeps bugging me to take some time—probably me away from her she means."

"Good! Done then. By the way, the Bledsloes are throwing an end of summer bash. You'll get to meet the mayor," Jack said.

Everett laughed. "I always wanted to meet a mayor, you know."

"I'll email you the when and where then. About a month from now? Pick you up at the San Fran International."

"Probably do me some good too. Get tired of looking at corn stalks all the time," Everett said.

When Jack snapped the phone shut, a great sense of relief washed over him as always does when confiding in a trusted friend. He drank his coffee and looked across the street. The white mist began to lift.

CHAPTER 9

It was Friday evening, meaning that not only the tourists would soon flock to Cannery Row, but the natives as well. All the shops would have been closed an hour or so ago as they already finished their abundant trade with the day travelers.

Unusually, Jack sat alone at Bully's, across from Sarge, who became less talkative as the server barraged him with orders, which seemed to progress exponentially. Bobbi must have been off tonight, he reasoned. He marveled, as a former student of The Hill, how Sarge could possibly keep up his regular military schedule at the language school by day and still tend to smucks like him four or five nights of the week. He remembered from his own days in the service that although the school courses began at 8:00 a.m., Sarge probably showed up for morning physical fitness two hours prior. Monday through Friday. During the last few weeks, Jack had also learned casually that the soldier/bartender was two credits away from his degree in business as well.

"How the hell do you manage that plate with all the bullshit the army puts you through?" he had asked on round two at the bar.

"Here and there," Sarge answered, shrugging his shoulders. "I started college courses just before my second re-up. Hell, Jack, it's not so bad. You've been in. Most of the enlisted spend more time on the other side of the bar than I do behind it. I don't wake up hungover every morning. Same time spent though. I just bettered the use of it. Figured it would help make rank since I was staying green for the duration. So I did a course here on the net and a course there in the classroom. Simple. By the time I got to DLI, the credits added up, and I found I was three classes away from my degree. Zeroed in and knocked one out at a time. This month finishes it—almost same time the language course ends."

"Ever hear of sleep, Sarge?"

"Sometimes," he laughed. "I get about five a night, first three days of the week. Studying Czech a few hours after work. Enough to get by the next day.

Thursday night I go to the community campus for my college course. Saturday, I study both. Sunday, I recover—a little. Just time management, that's all. I'm a NCO, so all the idiot details go to the lower enlisted. Sometimes I get called out and I just put a corporal in charge and I study at the desk. Stay under the radar mostly. I get it done—one week at a time."

"You're a machine."

"Nope, just want more than I got. You know, like your jackpot invention. I'm sure it took more than a day," Sarge concluded.

"Maybe one or two," Jack smiled. He remembered him and Everett in the wee hours of the morning in his basement. "Hey, Sarge, how about letting me buy you one of those Rummers you make for the rest of us? Off the record, of course."

"Sure, but don't squeal on it." Jack crossed himself and locked his lips, tossing the imaginary key over his shoulder, which indicated no squealing would be forthcoming. The bartender added the mixture discretely to his order. All drinks went to the server except one, which he grabbed and clinked Jack's glass before taking a long drag. He put it out of view under the bar.

"To self-made improvement. Thanks, Jack."

"Hear, hear," he answered. Tony had entered the bar in usual hurried fashion. He gave a quick mock salute to the bartender who returned with a barely negligible finger, and then plopped down next to Jack. Tony's breathing was harder than normal.

"Pitcher of the usual, Sarge. Bring it to the lounge, will ya?"

"Sure, Mr. Bledsloe," the bartender answered as Tony grabbed Jack's sleeve and left the barstool, ushering him away.

"What's the matter with you, Tony? You look like you've seen twin ghosts or something."

"Rough day. Goddamn audit is keeping everyone up late there. Pop is being a pain in the ass, like usual—personally going over every damn detail of everything. Like it's my first day behind the desk. I just cut out of the place a half-hour ago. Wants us all back tomorrow morning. At seven. Christ, I wish he'd retire."

"Everything alright?" Jack asked.

"Alright, alright. Sure it's . . . " Tony began, before being interrupted by the arrival of the Rummer en masse. Tony's eyes darted back and forth from Jack to the waitress.

"Bobbi's not here?" he asked.

"Nope. You're stuck with plain, old Janice, sweetheart. Why, were you looking for her?" she asked with a trace of snide, residing in those who are certain of immunity.

"Oh no, just curious," he said and hurriedly handed her a bill including a five-spot tip. "I got this one, Jack."

"Thanks, Mr. Bledsloe. I'll be sure to let Bobbi know that she was greatly missed," she said slyly and left the table.

"Oh . . . ok."

"You were saying, Tony . . . the audit?" Jack prompted.

"The . . . oh, yeah." He took a long drink and emptied a third of the glass before catching his breath. "Damn, that's at least still good. Yeah, the audit. These federal pricks. They come in with their wiry thin glasses and make a big to do, putting everyone and God through the strainer just to say they did. Nothing to worry about. But Pop is . . . you know. From the old school. Everything by the edited volume of yesteryear."

"Christ, Tony, I hope it's by the book if the feds are combing it."

"It is, it is," he answered, eyes darting again to the window. "Like I said, just a formality really. They should be wrapped up in a week. Bastards."

"That's good then."

"Yeah, it's good. Hey look, Jack, can I talk to you before anyone else shows up? I kind of need a favor, old boy."

"What's up, Tony?"

"It's no big deal really, but if Drew asks you, I need you to say I was with you last night. Till about midnight. I know Beverly wasn't there last night with you—you know, inside wife connection and all. Miles and one of his concubines bumped into the two of them last night at Cello's so they wouldn't have seen you around The Row. What do you say, buddy? Could you do me that? No one would know but us. Promise."

"Is it Bobbi?" Jack asked softly.

"Yeah, but . . ."

"Jesus Christ, Tony." Jack put his fingers to his temples and rubbed slowly.

"It's no big deal. You know? I just lost track of time. Little too much of Sarge's jungle juice. Hell, she served it to me, for Christ's sake. It was a one time thing,

Jack. Drew's gone ballistic. Thinks she has it all figured out. But we could smooth it over. If you were to just say . . ."

"It wasn't a one time thing, Tony, anyone can see that. I'm only surprised it took your wife this long to."

"She *suspects* it, Jack. But like my attorney says—what one suspects and what one can prove rarely resemble each other. Hence, your help, old boy. C'mon, Jack, she is threatening *divorce*. That shit I don't need."

"Why *don't* you just do it then? Divorce her, that is."

"How long you been here, Jack? A whole day? Let me clue you in. California law says she gets half. California law doesn't give a rat's ass of crap whether she's a bitch or not. And she is, Jack. A bitch. A spoiled rotten little bitch. You know it and I know it. But the law doesn't know or care to. Law says the bitch gets half the autos, half the house and half of the investments. She gets half of my goddamn golf clubs, if she wants. You think it's easy living with the goddamn constant harping? The prattling about her 'work' as if the fucking world would shut down if she didn't make gay day rounds that afternoon? Then on top of everything, she cuts if off anytime she wants. Like when in one of her pissy little snits, which might last a month. Easy to live with? It's not, Jack. But all I have to do is remember half—and I'm not talking about the better half. You know what I'm talking about, right, Jack? I bet her pal, Beverly, is already starting to act the same. She talks to Drew, you know. Thinks she already has you too."

Jack sat and said nothing.

"Ahh, just like I thought, Jacko. You're a smart guy. You watch me and Drew and see you and Beverly. Ten years later. We were like you once, Jack. *I* was like you. Football hero. Prettiest girl in my bed. Money. All of it. But that's how it is with these women, Jack. I'm telling you. They start small with their shit. Get their claws in your back until your nerves deaden. Eventually reach what's left of your spine until you don't feel anything anymore. Then they've got you, old boy. And you think you can just leave? Christ, Jack, most of them already have a lawyer on retainer before they even spit out 'I do.' So I'm stuck now. Far less money spent to just keep her. So what do you say, Jack? She'll be planning that stupid end of summer party soon and forget this shit. I'll have canned Bobbi by then so what do you say, old buddy?"

Jack put his fingers on the table and crossed them. "Alright, Tony . . . if she asks. I'm really not good at this sort of thing though."

"Just answer quick and casual. Tell her we were at Reginald's. On Alvarado Street. None of her cronies ever show up there," Tony said.

"Reginald's. Alvarado."

"Good man. Good man, Jack. Won't happen again," Tony said, raising his drink. The fruit rum mixture sloshed in the glass and overflowed the edge. He casually wiped it with the bar napkin and raised it again to Jack.

"Good man. Like I said, never will ask again," he repeated.

"I hope not, Tony . . . for your own sake."

"Hey, honey!" he yelled over Jack's ear, causing him to cringe slightly. "How about another pitcher. Right on my tab. My buddy doesn't have a tab tonight." Tony was instantly cheered and less nervous due to the effect of alcohol, Jack's compliance or both. They were beginning a third pitcher an hour later when Drew and Miles came in. Drew flopped down but kept herself across from her husband. Her eyes fixed on his briefly before she turned her attentions.

"My *dear* Jack. No Beverly tonight?" she cooed.

"Nope, gave her the night off from my antics," he said. She chuckled and looked across the bar, and then locked eyes into Jack's with a brilliant smile.

"It's always *splendid* to have a night off from things, isn't it? I understand you and my husband had a night off yourselves," she continued, radiating teeth, which masked the cold fire in her eyes. Tony's thoughts had retreated into the far corner of the lounge while Miles found recent fascination with the ceiling fan.

"Yep. Something like that," Jack replied quickly. *Christ, this is bullshit. She knows. She knows and is slapping around the mouse now—just because she can.*

"Really, my dear Jack—keeping my Tony out until the small hours. I didn't realize you had a habit of staying out so late on a school night."

"Just lost track of time, I guess. Tony is a pretty entertaining guy." The table echoed a fleeting laugh, followed by a louder hush.

"That he is. That's what I always say, do I not, dear . . . entertaining? To myself and others, of course. Now, where did you boys go again?" Drew said. The teeth closed to the shark's smile at the scent of chum.

"That new place. Or newer, I guess. Reginald's, you know, on . . . hell, what's that street, Tony?"

"Alvarado."

"That's it. Still not up on the lay of the land," Jack finished. He quickly took a drink to cover what he was sure appeared to be a spade shy of poker face between his ears.

"Oh yes, *Reginald's*. I do not believe I have ever been there . . . or should I say that Tony has never taken me," Drew answered, never leaving Jack's eyes.

"You should check it out," Jack said. He felt the end of the trial nearing.

"I most certainly should. Do tell me, dear Jack, what type of band was playing?" His face froze, realizing the trap but unable to free his leg as the hunter neared. His mouth forced words, which wouldn't come.

"You know, regular stuff. Wasn't paying attention really," he answered sheepishly. Tony's gaze suddenly fell, his head flopped into his hands.

"I see. Tony, may I have a word, dear?" Her husband got up and looked as pale as Jack felt—he knew he had given something away but didn't realize what. She led Tony far from earshot to the telephone booths outside the lounge area.

"Shit, Jack!" Miles exclaimed. "Reginald's doesn't cover a band!"

"Fuck . . . goddammit! How the hell was I supposed to know that? He put me on the spot like not even an hour ago with this shit!"

"Not your fault, buddy. Tony should have known better. This crap between him and Drew isn't about that girl . . . what's her name?"

"Bobbi. The server here," Jack said morosely.

"That's it. Pretty girl too. It isn't the girl though. They've hated each other for quite awhile now. Bobbi is just a symptom of a disease run its course," Miles concluded.

"Tony thinks she'll divorce him," Jack said.

"They should but they won't. Too much money to lose—for both of them. Drew doesn't want to live off a large stipend of a few hundred thousand dollars. She wants to be the wife of a millionaire. Which Tony will be when his father finally retires. She'll be pissed for awhile, but she won't leave him. You can count on that straight to their bank."

The couple returned with Drew's face tear-stained and Tony's expression blank. "Boys will be boys," she said. "And I must thank you, Jack, for such an enlightening evening. It's good to know who one can trust and who one cannot."

"Drew . . . " Jack started, but the words wouldn't emerge.

"There, there, my dear Jack. Jack, the grand inventor, suddenly placed in our own little world. Do you like our little world, Jack? It is simply a pleasure, is it not? Now, dear Jack, I do not blame you *too* much. My husband placed you in a difficult position. And of course, as I did. I'll be going home now," she finished, picking up her coat.

"I'll take you," Tony said.

"Oh, I think not."

"Drew, c'mon," he said as he reached for her.

"I said I THINK NOT!" she screamed, slapping his arm down on the table. Several other tables ceased in mid-sentence. Sarge glanced up as she composed herself. "Don't concern yourself, Sargie. I'm leaving, of course. Please put our bill on Jack's tab. I believe he has earned it tonight," she said, walking to the door. A loud slam followed.

"I should go after her," Tony said.

"No," Miles replied. "Let her be for awhile. It will blow over. Crash at my place tonight."

"Goddammit, Jack," he growled as his large body rose.

"Easy, Tony," Miles said, placing his hand toward him. "She already knew. She outguessed you and set Jack up. You should have given him a better story than that. You know how Drew is about details."

"Yeah," he said and slumped back into his chair. "Sorry, Jack. Too much for one day, I suppose."

"What are you going to do, Tony?" Jack asked.

"Christ, guys, what can I do? Miles is right. Let her cool off. It'll blow over."

"You really think so?"

"Sure, old boy." Tony leaned back and locked his large hands behind his head. "Yeah. Yeah it will. I forget my wife's nature. She wouldn't be happy with the set-tlement. She divorces me and I have to keep her standard of living. California law—like I told you, Jack. But in a few years I'll own the *whole* company. My stan-dard of living doubles. Nothing in the law says I have to double hers. Fuck her. Let her be pissed. She can go cry to her Darla-do-gooder friends. I have to deal with Pop tomorrow morning. How about we call it a night, fellas?"

"Fine by me," Miles said. "Little too much drama for my blood in one eve-ning." Tony and he left while Jack paid Sarge at the bar. *Too much drama for my blood as well.* He took a slow walk back down the dark shoreline as the waves beckoned him home.

CHAPTER 10

Jack sipped a lager from his fridge and paced back and forth, sinking his toes into the plush, white carpet of his spacious living room. His mind filled with the rushing anxiety of one who has committed an irrevocable social blunder with no tactful way to rectify the error. A gaffe of such magnitude was quite impossible to remedy and only erased through the imminent death of the offended or the offender fleeing to the other side of the country, never to return.

Goddamn Tony. It's his goddamn fault to begin and end with. Everett was right. Jack was angry. Angry at Tony's irreverent superficiality, which led to the event. Angry at Drew, Miss Monterey, charity caseworker for the slighted and socially downtrodden. Noble equalizer of the world. Who wouldn't leave her husband, even on grounds of adultery, if it meant cutting her till in half.

Drew can't live on half. That's what Miles had said. Tony's wife couldn't live on half. What did Tony say he made roughly? Three, four hundred grand a year? Half of that and still not have to lift a finger. Jack knew people in Illinois who made fifty thousand a year and worked fifty hours a week. But it was true. Tony would be a millionaire when he inherited the rest. Hell, he'd be a millionaire now if his wife didn't spend every cent of his take home.

Everett had quoted him months ago: *Difference between money bequeathed and money earned.*

That is exactly it. People raised on the parental dole, not even grasping of their wealth. Why doesn't everyone have it? They really think that. That somehow on their end of the field the bubble was centered on the level. And no worries of the future. Tony worked for his dad. Position and promotion bequeathed as well. He certainly wasn't going to get downsized. He couldn't even comprehend downsized. He couldn't comprehend Sarge, who would be thrilled for the rest of his life with an annual third of what Tony had. And what do they do? They still fuck it up. The Bledsloes and the cloned Bledsloes who run this town. They fuck it up. Then the fucker redirects the blow right into good old boy Jack's lap.

The doorbell rang. Jack closed his eyes while he stood motionless on the rug. He already knew who it was. Drew, being female, called in the fire support. The support, which would gather its force and target the aggressor in a massive air strike. *Not a quick death either,* he thought. He walked to the kitchen, reached into the fridge and drew another lager. While he popped the cap, he seriously considered to not open the front door at all. An oncoming barrage he was not in the mood for. The bell rang again with amplified tone, signaling impatience and anger transferred through the ringer to Jack's ear. Resigned, he ambled to the door, took a breath and opened it.

"I don't believe you." Beverly charged past almost shoving him into the wall.

"Look . . . Bev," he began.

"I just don't believe you," she interrupted. Jack threw up his hands and took a draught. He walked back to the living room. Seeing she probably wasn't in the mood for cuddling on the sofa, he flopped on the easy chair and waited for the first missile to land right on his head.

"Drew just called me. . . ."

"Go figure," Jack said. He almost laughed in spite of himself. Beverly stood silent for a minute in the well-known posture of an angry woman before continuing.

"As I said, before you *interrupted me* . . . Drew just called me. You tried to cover for Tony. You actually tried to cover for that bastard."

"What the hell was I *supposed* to do? Say yes, Drew, you are correct? Your sleuth technique is right on? Your husband is fucking the barmaid? Christ, Bev, give me a break!"

"Oh, what class, as usual. You could have just said nothing, you know. Changed the subject? Instead of *enabling* him."

"No, I *couldn't!*" Jack suddenly yelled. "My bud Tony already *told* her the story. Then he drops it on me about a nanosecond before she gets there. Then your pal grills me like some third-rate detective. If I had shut up, it would have confirmed what she already knew. They put me on the spot, Bev."

"No, that is incorrect, Jack. *Tony* put you on the spot. If only you had the integrity . . . "

"You know what, Beverly?" Jack said, cutting her off. "Maybe since Drew already figured it out, *she* could have just shut up instead of getting me involved. Instead of coming after me when she already *knew* the answer. But Drew can't ever just *shut up,* can she, Beverly! Christ, I can almost side with Tony!"

"Oh, so pardon me! It's all *Drew's* fault! My mistake entirely!" Beverly shouted.

"It doesn't help that she struts around like some pretentious, over-aged sorority girl. Mouthing off at everyone. If she knew about Bobbi, then she knew. Christ, Beverly, Tony wasn't all that subtle about it. Hell, Sarge was the one who told me."

"Sarge . . . the *bartender,* told you?" she asked, her tone growing softer.

"Yep," Jack answered.

"Well, that's just *perfect,* isn't it? It's horrible enough that Tony runs around like some junior high school boy reaching puberty, but now some *army bartender* has to publicize it. Why, Drew and I will go straight down there about this. We don't need someone like *that* causing problems in *our* community."

"Someone like what?" Jack said coolly. "An enlisted guy trying to make a living?"

"Just stop right there, Jack Strickland, with the *I came from the military and look at me now* crap. *I made my living the hard way so I know all!* You know what I mean."

"I'm afraid I don't, Beverly."

"Why, it's perfectly simple. You *made* something of yourself. A sign that you never should have had to wave around that silly salute anyway. Someone like Sarge though. Well, *look* at him, Jack. How old is he—thirty? Still marching around. I've met *officers,* you know. They are commissioned at twenty-two years old. There he is, a *grown* man, and he will answer to any fresh twenty-two-year-old. Why, he would have to stand at attention for him if they wanted him to, wouldn't he, Jack? Of course he would. If Sarge was going to *do* something with his life, he would have already *done* it. And he hasn't. Simple as that." She sat down on the sofa, crossed one leg over the other and looked at Jack with defiance.

"He happens to be a mid-level sergeant, Beverly. Probably in charge of forty young guys," Jack replied. His own voice grew icy.

"Ooooo, a *Sergeant!*" she laughed, holding her hands in feigned terror. "Forgive me for not recognizing *that* immense achievement for simply standing at attention like a trained pup for ten years. I've lived below The Hill long enough to know what a *mid-level sergeant* is. And it is not a Commander or Colonel, is it? Not someone who *runs* things. I know full well how military rank works, Jack.

There are officers and there are enlisted. He's enlisted. He could be a *high*-ranking sergeant and he's still enlisted. King of the Peasants. Saluting the first ensign he sees in your navy," she chortled. "Really, Jack, please."

"Actually, you're wrong, Beverly. He's not some stupid enlisted guy. And I guess I would know, being a stupid enlisted guy myself, according to you. He's one or two credits from a degree. Did you know that, Beverly? And he didn't have it handed to him on a gold platter like you and your people," Jack replied, finishing the beer. He went to the kitchen and started on another one. Beverly got up and followed him menacingly.

"A degree? From what—vocational school?" she sneered.

"Business. Finishing right here in your community college, I believe. While he's working and studying a foreign language. Probably bartending to pay for the bills that aren't covered by the army's huge paycheck. But you women here wouldn't know about that, would you? You look for men to cover those bills. Christ, Everett was right."

"I pay my . . ." she started.

"Yes, you work. Only until you find someone to relieve you from it. See the problem with people like you and Drew and Tony and probably Miles is you can't grasp a simple concept. That concept being that not everyone is born with what you have. And that you shouldn't mock those who weren't."

"Everyone has opportunity . . ." she tried to begin again.

"Oh yes, the platitude speaks. The Jaded Tower from the Ivy League. Everyone has opportunity. And yes, it is true, Beverly. The opportunity is there. For everyone. Your fault relies in the fact that you thumb your noses at those *engaging* the opportunity. You relish with those who never had to engage. Not for a single day of their lives. You were brought up *here,* Beverly. In the land of super-haves. You keep the gutter on the back rack in Seaside. If you truly understood the nature of opportunity, you wouldn't snub your nose at the ones pursuing it. And here's a clue, Beverly, the engagers of it usually start out with nothing. You and Drew never engaged. It was handed to you."

"I went to *college!*"

"Ah yes, your college years. What is that, Beverly? Thirty hours a week with study? Tops? You didn't major in medicine, for Christ's sake. *Or* engineering. You and Drew picked easy degrees while waiting to land the right man or should I say the right pay grade. So you can continue to have someone row you around in the lake of leisure. Unlike Drew, you never found yours at the university. Then as further insult you snub your nose at Sarge. And me—a long time ago. When I turned eighteen, I went to the navy because I didn't have the money for college. Simple. And I was turned down for a dance a long time ago by one of your own because of it. Not marriage, Beverly. A simple dance. Because that's how you think. *That's what you think!* When all of the lofty platitudes fall from grace, that's what you think. You just don't say it out of political correctness. And sometimes you do say it—in your own circles. If you people had an ounce of worldliness, you would be in awe of Sarge for what he is about to complete. I am. Because I've been there too. But no, you sneer at people like us, which are most of us by the way, Bev. Us mechanics and bartenders and God forbid, a man spending twenty years serving his country as a noncommissioned officer—or King of the Peasants, as you say. At least he has a job. How about you, Bev? Why are you pushing marriage so fast?" Jack sat down on the sofa and kicked his feet up on the ottoman, taking another long swallow from the bottle. He realized that in a minute or two he and Beverly were past tense. And he found it didn't bother him in the least. He took another swig and felt like he had just ducked prostate cancer.

"I'm warning you, Jack. I don't like your implication," she stated, pointing her finger at him. He looked at her and broke into a wide grin.

"Did you warn Miles too, Bev?" She grew suddenly quiet, finger now retracted to hip.

"That was a year ago. I didn't see the need to even mention it."

"Really?" he said as the grin transformed into a full laugh. "No need to mention it? How about mentioning that you moved in with him shortly after you started dating? Proposed matrimony to two soul mates in two years? What an incredibly fortunate girl you are, aren't you? Or maybe the more legitimate possibility is that you're more in love with marriage to money than to love. I'll bet Everett's kewpie that is exactly it."

"I don't have to have this conversation," she fumed and grabbed her pocketbook.

"Oh yes, you *do!*" he shouted. He rose and stepped in front of her. For the first time in his life he felt a rising want to slap the living hell out of a female. He took a breath as she stood motionless. "Really, I want to know," he said as his voice calmed. "What if I *wasn't* the inventor of some so so gadget, which just happened to go ape shit on the market? What if I were bartending—say at Bully's? Still interested?"

"Don't give me *that*! For Heaven's sake, Jack, people date in their own class. Is that so terrible? There, I've said it. Are you happy? And no, I certainly—*certainly* would not date some bartender. I happen to have a little more respect for myself than that, Jack."

"There you have it," he said. He circled around her and returned to the chair. Jack stared vacantly ahead and drank from the bottle. It was over. He had just broken up. Only thing left to do was to stab her a few times on her way out for good measure. "You're right. In your own class. And I'm a millionaire. You're not. So get out."

"You're tossing me away, are you?" she replied with a hint of mockery. "Are you sure, Jack?" Her eyes laughed at him as if she already had his replacement warming up on the deck. *And she probably does*, he thought. The simple fact was her looks would have another affluent guy's interest by the end of the week. And maybe he'd never see it coming either.

"You know what the difference between a Monterey girl and a hooker is, Bev?" he snorted. When she didn't answer, he continued. "The hooker's at least honest about the endeavor. I'll have your things packed in a box on the front door tomorrow. Now please leave."

"You're a son of a bitch, Jack Strickland. Nothing but working class that happened into money. You'll never be like us."

"You bet," he replied. She slammed the front door hard enough to vibrate the chandeliers. "You bet, sweetheart," he whispered. He got up and went to his giant refrigerator and drank another of what would be many beers that night.

CHAPTER 11

Two weeks had passed before Jack ventured back to Cannery Row. He had gone out of his way the last few weeks with his now nightly drinking to Salinas and Big Sur, sipping lagers leisurely at the resorts and cafes lined along the white sanded and rocky beaches. One weekend he had traveled up north along Route 1 to Bodega Bay, another smaller and less known version of Monterey. He drank an entire six-pack while he sat on top of Goat Rock in the gray twilight, watching the methodical rise and fall of two humpback whales in the distance. He spent another few days down south at San Simeon, walking back and forth the few miles between cliff enclaves, which enclosed the shoreline there. He drank Jamaican imports those nights at his hotel, which overlooked the water. Further south, he found Morro Bay. The seagulls gazed at the solitary man who consumed many margaritas at the dock's cafes and bars. He found there were many places where no one knew nor cared that Jack Strickland was the great inventor of the MAT. To their natives he was just a passing tourist like the other passing tourists. But mainly, he remained at home and visited only his lager while he watched listlessly from his large television. His nightly alcohol intake steadily increased as his spirits dissipated. He hadn't run in weeks.

But through the nightly intoxications, which dulled the edge from his recent breakup and the distancing from Tony and Drew, Jack, after carefully reviewing the summer, concluded an indisputable fact. And that pertinent truth, now sealed by his conscience, was he hadn't done anything wrong. Nothing to break their elevated social protocols. On the night of Tony's extra-curricular unearthing, Jack would have been the asshole no matter what he said, thanks to Tony who placed him in the predicament to begin with. In fact, the more he pondered it, the angrier he became. Once placed on hiatus from the Bledsloes, he began to loathe Tony's wife. Miles was correct. Drew wouldn't divorce Tony no matter what he did. Because of money. Nothing more or less. She would wait until Tony's father retired, which gave her a larger chunk of the pie. Jack almost could empathize with Tony's infidelity. Drew had the morals of a nicely manicured alley cat. She was not a good person. Which made Jack think further. Good people do not associate with bad people. And Beverly associated with Drew. Actually, Beverly was her best friend. And a best friend becomes one due to commonality. Which by axiom, equaled to the fact that Beverly was not a nice person. End product— Drew and Beverly were self-absorbed, spoiled brats. Gold diggers. Drew stamped her claim already and was not about to relinquish it. And she had attempted to get her friend the adjacent lot. Jack only considered himself fortunate he found out before Beverly drove the stake through. She had picked up her boxes left on his porch while he was on the shoreline path the morning after their altercation.

"Fuck 'em," he said to no one, bringing the thick hops to his lips. But he began to grow restless, flipping through four hundred channels of nothing worth watching. *Why in the hell should I have to hide anyway?* he reasoned. *If anyone should feel awkward it should be the Bledsloes.* He couldn't stay locked away like the Pope for the rest of his life. Fair or foul, he had not only reached their level on Monterey's societal rung of greatness, he had surpassed them. And unlike most of them, he had *earned* it. He had every right to sit among them. Besides, he hadn't seen Sarge for awhile.

He finished the lager in one defiant gulp, put on his jacket and headed for The Row. When he walked through Bully's door, he saw them. Tony, Drew and Miles sat with their familiar pitcher and three ice-filled glasses in the lounge. Jack gave a casual wave and ambled to the bar counter. It appeared that Sarge was off. He didn't recognize the bartender as working there before. He ordered a domestic draft and watched the darkened wheat liquid stream out into the side of the glass mug, angled with just enough expertise to create the perfect one-inch foam head on top. As he stared ahead, he felt a tap on his shoulder. When he turned, he faced Drew, who posed with a grand smile.

"Oh, dear Jack, you're not going to sit there by yourself, are you?" she stated.

"Just trying to keep the peace."

"Come now," she ordered, grabbing his arm and escorting him to the lounge. "Bring his drink!" she bellowed to the relief bartender who nodded and instantly came to the other side.

"Old boy, thought you decided to walk off the face of the earth," Tony said, shaking his hand, followed by Miles. Jack sensed only the tip of the iceberg begin-ning to thaw and shook his head no.

"How are you guys?" he asked.

"Us? Why we are splendid, just splendid," Drew pronounced. "Oh, don't worry, my dear Jack, all forgiven and forgotten. I was of course . . . snippy, Jack, but you do recognize the old adage of hell hath no fury . . . ?"

"No problem. Water under the bridge," Jack replied, anxious to change the subject.

"So, Jack," she began again. "You will remain to honor us at our end of sum-mer gala, will you not? Please tell me you have not made other reservations?"

"Sure, Drew, I'll be there. My buddy Everett might be down that weekend. Can I bring him?" he asked.

"You can bring anyone that you wish, my dear. Of course, I was hoping that you would bring Beverly. She tells me you haven't called her in weeks."

"I'm afraid that's over. It all went too fast, Drew," Jack explained, catching a side glance from Miles. He swore that his eyes were laughing at him.

"Oh, such a shame, such a grand shame. You two made such a *lovely* couple. But one never knows about these things, does one? Perhaps all that is needed is a cooling off? She is such a *fabulous* girl, is she not, Jack?" Drew probed. *Which translates to Beverly's temper cooled off and she realizes her hand got called. Sure, she wants me back. Just like Drew wants Tony. Maybe I should confirm the whole deal by running off with the waitress,* he thought.

"Maybe, I don't know," Jack replied.

"And I'll put in my best word, of course," Drew said.

"Thanks." He wanted to drop the matter. They sat with their pitcher and lager, the tension now officially cut into pieces and placed in the storage box.

"So you guys are ok?" Jack asked.

"We are simply *marvelous,*" Drew answered, patting Tony's hand. Tony looked away slightly, and then nodded in agreement that marvelous was indeed what they were at the moment. "People go through these things, of course—not a perfect world. Look at the earrings Tony just bought me, Jack. Aren't they sim-ply exquisite?" Jack, as well as Miles, confirmed that they were exquisite. "And tomorrow we are going to begin shopping for my brand new Jaguar. Isn't that right, dear?"

"You bet," Tony answered with exactly one-fifth of Drew's enthusiasm.

"So where's Sarge?" Jack asked. "Usually he's on with the weekend."

Drew stiffened and let go of her husband's hand. "Sarge will not be around here anymore, I'm afraid."

"How come?"

"Why, I spoke to the owner, of course. Tony and I know the owner personally, Jack. And we all agreed that it was in everyone's best interest if Sarge was terminated from his position." She leaned on her husband's arm slightly as the triumphant, radiant smile spread across her mouth. Jack's own mouth descended with his falling jaw as he stared at her.

"Drew . . . you've got to be kidding?" he said incredulously.

"I certainly am *not* kidding. I rarely tease, Jack. We prefer *our* bartenders in Monterey to serve drinks in lieu of gossip. Of course, my dear husband has accepted full responsibility for his role in the event, but we do not appreciate at all Sarge's intrusion in the matter. So Sarge is no more, you see," Drew said. She looked away and waved to someone outside of the window while taking a mouthful of the drink.

"Holy shit," Jack said. "You actually got him fired."

Drew's head returned from the window. The teeth had protruded into the shark's smile. The actual Drew Bledsloe emerged from the pseudo titles of community volunteer and societal wife. Unfeigned and authentic was the woman who sat across from Jack, her teeth shimmered like the blue bay, which held its sea monsters below the surface. The woman who would go to any length and use her position to fire an already not prosperous man. Purely for spite. "Oh, not just him, Jack. That little waitress tramp as well. And I made the owner promise to notify the other lounges and restaurants in the area of their recent endeavors. They won't be employed in Monterey any time soon, I'm afraid. Maybe in Seaside— where that sort of class belongs to begin with."

So this is how they work, Jack thought. *Really work, underneath their velvet and handshakes and pats on the back. Their class. Hell, now they're my class. They tell one of their foremen to fire the laborer and he does. Christ, Sarge has kids. He probably needed that job. And they took it. Took his wife and kids' money right out of his pockets. All out of pure meanness.* Jack sat with his hands clenched beneath the table.

"Should we get another pitcher?" Tony asked cheerily. "Just as good as Sarge's. Why, we'll toast to him, Jack. How about that? Final toast to old Sarge boy."

"No, dear," Drew interrupted. "I'm afraid we have an early morning tomorrow, Jack. At the dealer's, of course. We must be running along now. Tony, please pay the bill. Pick up Jack and Miles' tab as well." Tony dutifully went over to the bar counter as Drew gathered up her purse and straightened her blouse. "Well, Jack, I am certainly glad we have patched things up so nicely. Please do not be a stranger anymore," she said. She gave him a European kiss on the cheek, and then rounded the table and did the same to Miles. "Toodle loo boys. We'll see you tomorrow night?"

"Yeah, maybe," Jack replied.

"Oh now, don't be a sourpuss, dear Jack. I'm sure you'll find another Sarge. Sarges are a dime a dozen up on The Hill. Goodnight boys." She exited grandly as Tony waved and took her arm. The door shut behind them and left Miles who stared into Jack's eyes with bitter amusement.

"Like the lady not so subtly stated. Hell hath no fury and all. Note she is finally getting her Jag. What the hell can Tony do? Easier than a settlement in court. Legal fees alone are more expensive than one car in the end."

"He doesn't look too happy," Jack said.

"She's punishing him, Jack. Not just the car and earrings either. Last few weeks her credit has gone wild too. And there's nothing he has to say about it. But that's not all of it. The feds are raking him over the coals," Miles explained.

"I thought Tony said it was nothing."

"It's never nothing when those guys show up, Jack. He doesn't say much, even to me, you know, keeping appearances and all. But I'm starting to wonder if he's in trouble of the not so nice kind. They're running a second audit on his dad's company."

"Christ. I guess what comes around goes as well," Jack said.

"Yeah, maybe. Karmic payback for one's misdeeds and all. Zen Buddhism invades the high life of Monterey," Miles replied sourly.

"I still can't believe that Drew got Bobbi and Sarge fired though," Jack said. "Well, Bobbi maybe since she did plop her foot in the pie right in front of Tony's own wife, but Sarge?" Miles held a finger to his temple as his eyes narrowed.

"You have to be careful here, Jack. Maybe you don't because you're not tied to

Monterey financially. But all the business folks are. Shop owners, restaurant proprietors and even the mechanic who Drew talks down to on the corner. And I've known Drew a long time, Jack, and know how she is. You should see what Tony says behind closed doors. He told me the other night he can't believe you've held your tongue as long as you have—especially since you're an ex-military guy and all. No reason for you to stay in check. Not like all of her cronies. Now, don't take this the wrong way because I don't consider myself a snob. I was born here, raised here and pretty much had it handed to me on a shiny platter. And so did Tony. We know that. Which is good since I don't think I have the constitution to fight out of the muck like you did, Jack."

"You would if you had to, Miles," Jack replied.

"But I *didn't* have to. Like I said, I get it. And I see what's what too. Bottom line is that things run here the way they run. Sarge was a bartender. Tony and Drew do a lot of business here at the lounge. And they have a lot of friends who do as well. Lot of luncheons, liquid company meetings and all. Lot of business when things are slow and the tourists are back in their rat nests, curled up for the winter. So what do you think that the owner was going to do when Drew marched over in a tizzy and threatened to pull her crew? And that implies the threat of using her position in the community as well. She would never say that, mind you. We *never* say out loud what strings we could pull. It's all nice and cordial. She told him her version of what happened and her displeasure of the whole event. And her displeasure might just very well involve a surprise visit from the fire marshal in two months if Sarge didn't get the pink slip."

"Drew threatened that?" Jack asked.

"Nope. Like I said and she said. She never threatens. *We* never threaten. All sweet and all nice—but the point was made in-between hugs and hellos. And that, my transplanted friend, is how things are here down by the sea. For me too, Jack. What do you imagine happens if I rub the right people the wrong way?" Miles asked.

Jack sat back and breathed a heavy sigh. "Miles, do you ever wish you just worked in a factory on some mindless line?"

"Sometimes. But I *do* like the money. I will be the only native to admit it out loud, being the statement is uncomfortable to the other locals. You're not supposed to say you love it. And I do. I thoroughly enjoy being well off with my martini brunches by The Bay. I admit it. Too soft. I don't know any other way. I get one hundred and fifty thousand dollars a year from the city for a job I inherited after punching the Ivy card like the rest of them. A position that doesn't require much. I get a lot more in . . . well, other contributions. Factory guy doesn't get that. So I kiss the upper asses too."

"At least you do admit it," Jack said and toasted his lager glass towards him.

"And I'll reveal something else too, Jack. Only because I like you and all. You've done something that none of us can hold a candle to. You're *self*-made. A poor guy, and I'll judge you were a poor guy since you enlisted, right? My general understanding is that rich kids don't enlist?"

"I was poor," Jack confirmed.

"So a poor guy returns to the toil ground of his youth, now very wealthy, years later in our Camelot. And let me tell you, Tony and Drew can't stand it. Well, at least Drew can't. I can stand it because like I said, I already admitted that I know I'm soft. Soft childhood, soft schools, softer colleges and soft post-college. But most of these people around here don't like to admit that fact—even too themselves. Because to admit it is to say that they are living in a position they never earned or deserved. That Drew will drive her Jaguar off the lot tomorrow afternoon, not by perseverance or triumphant success, but by nothing more than pure luck. Luck of being born a pretty girl in a pretty society and sent to a prettier college in the east, which placed her in position to marry into more money. Luck of when and where she was born. Nothing more. The root origin from the tree's highest branches of white guilt. Then they have to believe it is not only luck but destiny. People are placed where they are placed and nothing they can do about it. Crack head was predestined in the ghetto, and Tony was preordained to run his father's company. Their justified fate. It eases their guilt to believe it was all just destiny. Then you come along with your self-made millions. And it drives right through their hearts how worthless they all really are. And we are, of course. But I'll never admit that one outside of this table." Jack raised his hands signifying the confidence.

"Oh, one other thing, Jack. Don't think for a second Drew wouldn't hurt you if she could. Unfortunately for her, you have no one to answer to here. You can sit on your bay-lined porch and suck Rummers down all day and there isn't a damn thing she can do about it," Miles said.

"Why would she want to hurt me?" Jack asked.

"Revenge for her friend. Her best friend, mind you. Drew practically had Beverly drawn for her adopted sister-in-law."

"Miles, I have one question on that one."

"What's that, Jacko?" Miles asked, knowing the inquiry as a grin formed on his face.

"You never married Beverly. Why?"

"Ah, I was wondering if the rumor mill had finally sent you that package. You have completely broken it off with her?" He made a violin motion with his hands.

"Seriously, Miles, how come?" Jack asked.

"The whole truth and nothing but?"

"Yep."

"Because I've been there before. I also spent years watching Tony. And I didn't want to *end up like him.*"

CHAPTER 12

On the walk along the shoreline path back to his home, Jack stopped by his cove. He listened to the quiet rush of the darkened waters crash methodically in the low tide as the moon shone on the foam. He contemplated whether cannery workers used to stop and look into The Bay in the Steinbeck era as he did today. *Probably not,* he thought. *Most likely they were too exhausted from the long days and late evenings down The Hill.* Although it was a poor community in the cannery days, the class system still existed. Only the discrepancy was larger. There were the owners of companies and there was everyone else. The Bledsloes were the same Bledsloes back then, as of today. And the cove gave preference to none of them. The workers and masters now shared the same earth, all disintegrated into the dust they once stood on. And a hundred years from now, Jack, Miles, Tony, Drew and Beverly would share that same dirt as well.

It made Jack ponder on the triviality of man. His self-made notion of grandeur as if the riches somehow gave lease to added life. Mankind had been roaming from his cave approximately ten thousand years. The average lifespan of the cannery man was sixty-five to seventy. The average lifespan of modern Monterey man was only slightly longer, comparatively. Then *poof*—the decomposition process begins. One hour after the heart ceases to send blood downrange.

Even the rapidity of the lifespan for those who surpass all averages and graduate the Reaper's course at the top of the class. Just a few more added years. Childhood, which drags kicking and screaming into adolescence, which stands its ground, until adulthood claims it. Then starts the slow walk, accelerating quickly into a sprint towards death. Everyone was the same. That was the cosmic joke that Miles, Beverly and the Bledsloes didn't get. The universe lets no one out alive.

Jack, even today, was sometimes still angered by the community perception of Young Jack over a decade and a half ago by the natives. At the same time, he wrestled inwardly that he only wished to be a part of them. He had envied their luck of being born into the design class of grand houses and grander thoughts. It was possible that the inner turmoil at the pub with the girl so many years ago was not his dismay at her rejection but the subconscious belief that she was correct in the judgment. From a lowly seaman, who took orders from those who sometimes didn't even hold a high school diploma, grew his motivation to rise not only above the dull petty chiefs and even more obtuse officers, but to launch himself in the midst of those who once ridiculed his white cap. He had visions at eighteen of one day coming down Highway 1 in a sporty car, top down, past the sands of Marina Beach, past Seaside and down Del Monte Avenue. He would get that dance then, he had visualized.

When he acquired his engineering degree, he thought about moving to the coast, but then upon a few hours with the net's cost calculator, he realized that sixty thousand a year grants a sparse paycheck to paycheck existence in places like Monterey. And Jack didn't want to return sparse. He wanted to return magnificent. He forgot about the coast while he and Everett pursued their hobby, which transformed into an invention, which cultivated into a wealth that Jack could never have imagined, even in his enlisted reveries. He had made the decision to buy a house in Monterey abruptly. The device had sold and manifested tremendous profits within months for the two young inventors. Jack, long quit of his engineering position a few years later, was bored one morning, rearranging the items in various storage boxes in his basement when he came across his old uniform in a clear plastic bag. It still had the Third Class Petty Officer rank of his discharge sewn to the shoulders. He remembered he had pressed and folded it neatly that day as he left Norfolk, his permanent duty station between voyages after language school. And the surge suddenly hit him. Why not? He had not been to Monterey since he left The Hill. He couldn't think of a better place to launch into early retirement while he gazed at the sea from the lofty residence at the bottom of The Hill instead of on top. But, it was something else, which only now did he realize. The old gnawing wound, which he left The Bay with the first time. Jack had wanted to *show* them, although he couldn't hand pick exactly who "them" was. So he got online and convinced himself it was for amusement only when he looked at real estate in the area. Then for further entertainment, he called the number of the agent. Within a few minutes he found himself talked into flying out there to look around. A short time later found one Jack Strickland sitting in his paid off house, looking at the shoreline path to Lover's Point, which he had frequented so many years ago.

He had no inclination to visit his old alma mater on top of The Hill. He wanted to present himself to the locals. The new and improved Jack Strickland, years and far removed from white duckies and lined formations. The *rich* Jack Strickland. That was why he went to Bully's. Although modest by nature, he knew eventually his financial status would be revealed. And he *wanted* them to know.

He wanted to dance.

And Monterey, the side of Monterey, which had been blocked off to him in his youth, now welcomed him with open arms. His thoughts and opinions now mattered to the locals. They meant something. He *meant* something. The elite now wished for his patronage. Drew and Tony. Miles. And his time with Beverly was only icing on the cake.

It is the trivial and superficial that is the least difficult to conceal, the deeper core becomes more visible as the social drills continue their relentless penetration of the shiny outward surface. It was apparent that Drew was not the least bit in love with her husband and was more angered by her tarnished image than of Tony's infidelity. It was also evident that she was using his indiscretions for her own means as she used everything else. A Jaguar. One adulterous affair patched up with a Jag and a set of earrings. Jack had come to the recent conclusion that his youthful perceptions of the better class were greatly artificial. The Monterians weren't a better class. They were just a wealthier class. They didn't settle differences with their fists, like his dad used to tell him of Uncle Pete's bar in Illinois. Their weapons were softer, yet lethal to those directed toward.

Like Drew's revenge on himself. She didn't get rid of Sarge at Bully's because she was mad at Sarge for blurting out what her husband was doing. Any other woman would have been enraged with the female culprit, not the messenger. A normal woman would have thanked Sarge for letting it slip. She knew he and Sarge were chums. She was getting even with him. Not just for dropping Beverly either. She took revenge on him for pumping tainted blood into the general circulation and having the audacity to step across their velvet rope.

And yet she maintained the social decorum of civility, even amiability towards him. *Because that's how they do things here,* he thought. The reign of appearance over feeling. They needed him. He was higher on the social ladder than they were. In a twisted way, with all their money and large houses, they still needed him. To validate their importance. Ironically, he now made them feel as inadequate as they made him feel years ago. And they were too dim to realize how pointless it all was. Their heightened social diversions, conditioned probably since they could walk the shoreline. They would grow old just like Joe the mechanic. Drew would grow old. And then no one would care if she was rich.

But in the meantime she took Sarge's job. Didn't really matter much, Jack supposed, since Sarge was leaving soon for his permanent station, but it was still money to him that he probably could have used. And one of Jack's acquaintances took it from him. All because she had a husband who was semi-wealthy.

Suddenly, as he stared at the dimly lit waters and the sun, which had well crossed the foothills of Big Sur, Jack realized he despised these people. He had no common ground with any of them. He was only a novelty. It was only his presence near them that elevated their own state. And, of course, Drew had noted him for fund raising on her asinine future projects. If Jack Strickland, the new neighbor, made a mere sixty thousand a year, he would have indulged alone at Bully's last May.

Everett. Thank God Everett was to arrive the weekend of the Bledsloe bash, which ended the summer. Jack didn't even want to go. But he was committed now. Even the individualist has to occasionally participate in forced societal norms in order not to be strung from the nearest line. But he decided that after their festivity, he was going to vanish from Drew and Tony altogether. Drew probably wanted him distant as well. And Tony was too numb to care. And that was fine. He was drinking too much anyway these last months. If he kept it up, like when with the Bledsloes, (which until recent had been nightly) he would be an alcoholic soon. So he would go with Everett, he concluded, stay a few proper hours and leave the Bledsloe clique for good. All for form's sake. Things would have been handled differently in his uncle's bar back home.

Everything would have been different back home.

CHAPTER 13

September

"I can smell the seawater already," Everett said as they merged from Highway 101 into 1, which led toward the coastline.

The big event came on the second weekend of September. Most of the tourists had children, due in school by then, which left only a few last minute stragglers on the streets of Monterey. By October, the cool mist would rest only on the natives. Jack had picked up Everett at the San Francisco airport, but this time, in lieu of an expensive hotel, he took him to his home on The Bay.

"Just over the sand dunes," Jack said, enjoying his role as tour guide. "Other side of the water is M-town. I can even see from this end of The Bay where I live."

"Really?" his friend exclaimed. "Let's pull over here first and take a looksee. See if we can find your house." Everett's childlike excitement amused Jack as he pulled into the Marina State Park, after grabbing a six-pack from a food store. *Probably more stimulating than looking at his field back home,* Jack mused. They got out of the car and made their way over the sliding sand dunes and with first beer opened, gazed at the lights from The Wharf and The Row across the dark water.

"Toward the left is Fisherman's Wharf. Right of that is Cannery Row. I live about a mile—right from where Cannery ends. We'll walk there tomorrow if you like," Jack said.

"Yep, I like." They stayed at the dunes for a half-hour before Jack took the remaining beer and Everett, who was much lower on tolerance, back on the last few miles of the highway to his house, where they finished the rest.

The next morning Jack walked Everett down the shoreline path to Lover's Point and back through Cannery Row to The Wharf, where they devoured a seafood luncheon. Full and tired, they stopped on the way back at Bully's.

"I see why you wanted to come back here," Everett reflected when they sat down. "This place *is* Eden. So what's the cost of living anyway?"

"Rent or own."

"Both."

"You can rent for about seventeen to eighteen hundred a month in most places. Houses in the near area start around five hundred thousand," Jack explained.

"Whew. No wonder everybody has the elitist complex you talked about. A small six figures sits you in the poorhouse, I imagine."

"Yeah . . . just ask Drew and Tony sometime," Jack replied.

"Ah, your friends," Everett said.

"Not so much lately." Jack relayed the past events of the last few weeks while Everett slowly shook his head.

"So he gets a little poochie, she gets a car and all's even-stevens? Lord, Jack, Shirley would have had me in divorce court before the next sunup, even if she had to wake up the judge in the small hours. Invention or no invention."

"Yeah, you'd think. Fact is, Everett, I don't think Drew even wants me at her party at all. But there's no socially correct way for either of us to get out of it. Tony's still ok with me, but I think she is still really pissed," Jack said.

Everett laughed. "You sure know how to step in the middle of the cow pie, Jack. Be an interesting night to look at though. And this girl of yours. You're kaput with her too?"

"Afraid so."

"Oh well then. To better friends," Everett said, raising his glass. Jack clinked it and took a swallow. None of the clique was in today. The Bledsloes were probably preparing for Monterey's grand social gathering of the exceedingly privileged. He emptied his glass quickly and felt that he might need a few more to prepare himself as well.

◆ ◆ ◆

Everett and Jack arrived at the Bledsloes at 8:00 p.m. It was Saturday night and the air gave all indication that it would remain clear for the duration of the night's event as if even Monterey weather arranged itself around Tony and

Drew's summer affairs. Jack was instantly uncomfortable as he entered the door. Several guests stared. While Drew introduced the two, he wished he were at his own window, watching the blue waters turn gray as the sun faded over the foothills.

The Bledsloes owned a six-bedroom house, which Jack found odd as Drew had emphatically stated her lack of desire for future generations. The grass on their five-acre lawn was trimmed neatly and evenly matched the spotless interior of the inside of their house. There was not a grain of dust anywhere that Jack could hold witness to, from the polished marble foyer to the gleaming kitchen, where Drew had multiple caterers busily following her array of orders. The living room was filled with guests.

Jack realized the root of his tension the minute Tony had answered the door. He could tell from long acquaintance that he had been at the punch for some time. Jack looked to Everett as to apologize silently as his friend hadn't noticed yet their immediate error.

"Goddammit, Drew," Tony yelled to the kitchen after giving a quick nod. "Didn't you tell them the dress?" He was in a full tuxedo as were the other guests. Drew scurried out.

"Oh my, this is my fault, of course. I thought you mentioned it, dear," she chatted pleasantly while smiling directly at Jack. "No matter—you two look dazzling. And this must be your friend, Everett, which Jack has told so much about. Please disregard my husband's lack of tact. Welcome to our home, boys. This is Tony and as Jack well knows, I am Drew Bledsloe."

"This is Everett Coffman," Jack said. He flushed as he examined the other penguins in the room. Everett fidgeted as well as people do if accidentally forced into a position of nonconformity. *I bet she did that on purpose,* he thought viciously, feeling pauperish in his six hundred dollar suit.

"Sorry," he muttered in Everett's ear as Drew led them to the vast living room.

"At least I'm not the only one," Everett snickered. *See, he doesn't care,* Jack reflected. *Everett could have come in a T-shirt and shorts and wouldn't have a care worth of less about everyone else. Few months ago you wouldn't have either, old boy.*

Drew led them from one group to another in the already highly intoxicated room. Several of the tuxedo ties hung off to the side of their owners' collars. The last couple she introduced to them consisted of a gorgeous woman hanging on the arm of her bald companion, whose tailor-fitted attire could not hide his lack of enthusiasm for the treadmill.

"Everett and Jack, this is Robert and Beverly. Of course, Jack, you are already acquainted with Beverly," Drew said, the smile evolving into the shark's teeth that signified the completion of her mission.

"Pleasure to meet you, Everett . . . hi Jack," Beverly said, instinctively pulling Robert closer who only stood with a nod and grin.

"How've you been, Bev?" Jack said, now extremely regretful of not being in his own living room, drinking beer with Everett. He hadn't seen her since she stormed out of his house. Upon looking at her, he realized one of man's great truths—that being of woman growing magically more attractive the second one sends her on her way.

"Beverly," she chided. "And I've been just fabulous."

"Robert owns several banks in the area. Always a major contributor to my organization," Drew said merrily.

"Just doing the old nine to five like everyone else," Robert chuckled.

"Oh, such modesty for such a key figure in the city. Well, I'll let you boys run off alone now to mingle at your leisure," Drew said pleasantly but with sharp victory in her eyes that exchanged looks with Beverly. She disappeared into the crowd.

"You want to walk around, Everett?" Jack asked rhetorically.

"I reckon."

"Nice meeting you, Rob," Jack said, shaking his hand.

"Robert, it's Robert."

"Ok, Robert. See you around . . . Bev," Jack replied as Everett stifled himself.

"Nice seeing you again, Jack," she answered cordially. Jack and Everett went outside to the patio and second open bar as Everett erupted into a full gale of laughter.

"Now *that* was less than comfortable. Nice looker though."

"Yeah, yeah," Jack said. "You want anything special? I guarantee they can make it."

"Just a beer."

"Two then," he said to the bartender who was also dressed in a tuxedo. "Can't let my friend escape Monterey without trying the local lager, now can we?" The bartender reached in a back cooler and retrieved two bottles. He popped the caps while eyeing the attire of the two standing before him. Jack no longer cared. He counted the appropriate minutes needed to complete the social task before he could shoot out of the front door with Everett and head for The Row. Jack took a long draught from the bottle.

"I'm going to need about eight of these," he said.

"Lordy, what was all that about, anyway? I could have cut the tension with a hacksaw in there," Everett said.

"That was elite class warfare. If they can't put you out, at least they can make you feel like you are," Jack replied.

"That Drew is *not* a nice woman. No wonder her guy drinks, like you said. And not telling you about the dress code. Not that I care much since *I'll* never see these people again." Everett slowly became angry, not for himself, as much as for what he now saw his friend put through these last few months.

"I think after tonight I'm not going to see much of them either, Everett."

"How'd you get roped in with this crowd anyway?"

"It's funny," Jack said. "I never even knew I was tugging the line. Just people I met one night at the bar I took you to. I kind of grew on them, I guess. Don't know why. I don't have any common ground with any of them."

"Check your pocketbook again. No one dislikes millionaires," Everett concluded.

"You know, I got treated not so great here when I was in language school, all those years ago. It bothered me a lot—being a kid and all. But, there were a lot of hell raisers up on The Hill. The not so civilized types. Probably still are—up there. I figured if I came back and got to know the locals, it would be different. Figured people were just people, and they were just a different set. Turns out they are different people altogether. They are born here without a care to worry about. They go to their upper scale schools, learn about racism when they are all white. About poverty when they live in the suburbs. About the military when they've never worn the uniform. They are taught their views are valid because they are backed by Robert's bank. I guarantee not one of them in this room has ever worked a construction job, even for a summer. So I come along with the right credit but not the right credentials. It makes them uncomfortable—a reminder they didn't earn theirs. Miles was right," Jack finished. He looked at the crowd, which rapidly grew drunker by the minute. Beverly stole glances out of the side of her eye as she pulled her new companion to her.

"Money bequeathed versus money earned," Everett reminded gently. "The two parties aren't cut out for pals. Nothing in common."

"I think so, Everett. And I don't think the two parties can even get along. Hey, let's set our watches. I say another two hours is socially acceptable to cut out gracefully, don't you? Go back to my place and open the windows and some bottles. Toast The Bay. Forget these people. Then tomorrow morning, nice and hungover, talk about our next modification."

"Modification?"

"Sure. Or next gadget. Just because I'm rich doesn't mean I'm not an engineer at heart. So are you, remember? Just like old times except no pesky forty-hour work week to interfere."

"Now that sounds just fine," Everett replied. "No pressure this time. Just a couple of inventors toying around. Why wait until tomorrow? How many hours?"

"Two," Jack said, tapping his watch. "Go grab a couple more from the bartender."

"You go," Everett countered. "I'm going to take a walk around this mansion. Be back in a few." They parted as Jack made his way to the inside bar.

"So what do you think?" he asked the bartender.

"About what, Sir?"

"About all this," Jack said, waving his hand across the living room.

"They're fine, Sir."

"Really? I think they're all a horse's ass too," he said and laughed, remembering Sarge while almost compromising the present barkeep who handed him a second lager. He sat alone. It took a few minutes before Beverly came over.

"So anyone new?" she asked.

"Nope. Obviously you rebounded just fine."

"Oh, he'll do, I suppose. Jack Strickland, if you're going to fit in here, we might want to work on that common demeanor. It just doesn't become you. Or then again, perhaps it does."

"You should go, Bev. Your bank is getting jealous," Jack said, jerking his thumb toward Robert across the room who watched the two intently with scrunched eyes. She narrowed hers.

"You know what, Jack . . . "

"Goodbye, Beverly." She sat several seconds, and then stood up and straightened her dress downward. A moment later she returned to Robert and was enthusiastically talking to several people. *Good God, I could have married that. I almost feel sorry for old Rob.* He looked at his watch. A half-hour had passed. *Screw it. I don't even want to be here or with them. And since exactly when do I do what other people want me to for social sake? I'm a goddamn millionaire. And they'd better get used to it. Let me find my bud and we are out of here.* He took a large gulp, and then left the beer and a twenty dollar tip for the bartender. As he got up, he heard a raised voice across the large room that sounded like it belonged to Everett. "What the hell . . . " he muttered to himself as he made his way through the crowd. Sure enough, the voice led to his friend who stood about a foot away from Drew.

"Oh, Jack," he said. "Sorry buddy, but I've had about as much as I can take here. Your friend Drew was just explaining to me the finer points of our lack of sophistication."

"I simply stated . . . " she began. Jack could tell by the summer's experience that Drew, like her husband, was quite intoxicated. And generally when quite drunk she transformed into quite mean. *Or isn't it true that she was already mean? The outside shells of nicety . . . all soluble with enough parts of Merlot added to the mixture.*

"I simply stated, " she bellowed again. "That *most* people—most *educated* people wouldn't have to be told the difference between a formal and non-formal gathering. I *did* mention, Jack, that it was a *formal* gathering, not some after work get-together at the union bar."

"*Educated?*" Everett shouted. "Holy moly, Jack, this one is something else. In case you haven't heard, Jack and I didn't just fall into the leprechaun's chest one fine day. We're *engineers*! That means we didn't have *time* for coffee shops or college fraternities or whatever you upper society types do for four years on your daddy's tab! We were too busy solving a differentials problem that might take a few days! Or a week! You know how many engineering students make it through? Not a lot. It seems to me that *you're* the one about two or three heads lower on the totem pole, honey!" Jack had never seen Everett angry like this. *Because she insulted him. Insulted him and his upbringing. Just like they insulted you the first week with their monologues about The Hill. Difference was you sat there and took it.*

"For *your* information, I attended the sister university to *Yale*! But I'm quite sure you know *all* about Yale, now don't you? " Drew shouted back, now deliberately trying to gain the attention of the crowd. She didn't need to as the gathering had stopped and silently stared, including her husband. Jack began to grin. *Go, Everett. That's exactly how I should have handled her the first day with that rotten crack about The Hill and the military. How was this woman my friend?*

"Oh sure, the rich young woman's prep for the marriage mill," Everett continued. "Where you spend a few years lying in wait for some poor rich boy to lock down his bank account forever. Tell me, honey, have you ever even had to work once in your life?"

"I have a job now for your information."

"Right, Jack told me about that one. Of course, it's not really a job, now is it? You've never really had a *job,* now have you? Your *husband* has a *job.* See, he pays the bills—pretty *large* bills from what I see here, I reckon. That would be the definition of a job. Something that takes your time in exchange for earned money. What you have is save-the-whales or whatever you and the other snotty housewives want to save. You have a hobby. Because you have too much time on your hands living off someone else's labor. You're not even raising kids, for God's sake. Probably because that's too inconvenient for you too. You're above all that, I reckon. But you know what you really are, lady? Under all this glit? You're a *parasite!* Nothing more than a loafing, stuck-up, rotten, little *brat!* Sorry, Jack, but I don't take that from *anyone!*"

"TONY!" she yelled, although her husband stood only ten feet away. "Are you going to just sit there and let him speak to *me* like *that!*" Tony began to move forward, his fists clenched towards Everett who stepped one foot back in preparation. Tony, who had been drinking since early afternoon. He stomped past Everett and up to his wife.

"You're *Miss Independent* so why don't you figure it out, Drew. Besides, you started on him. On both of them. You and your bitch of a friend. And everyone let's you get away with it. Insulting everyone, lecturing everyone and generally being a royal pain in the ass. And you wonder about the waitress? I wonder what took me so long. Hell, I'm apt to buy Jack's friend here a case of the good stuff." He turned and gave Everett one thumb up as he began to walk away. Drew forgot about Everett and rushed past him, toward Tony.

"You! How *dare* YOU speak to me in that manner in front of everyone! And I *marvel* how, after all of your escapades, you even *begin* to have the notion of self-righteousness. TONY! STOP WALKING AWAY FROM ME! DO NOT TURN YOUR *BACK TO ME!*" She shuffled behind him and grabbed the shoulder of his shirt. In one fluid motion, Tony whirled around and slapped her across the face. The loud crack was heard in the dumbly silent room as the Bledsloes' guests, friends and enemies stood with eyes widened and jaws dropped. Drew reeled backward before she fell into a comfort chair behind her.

"Holy Christ," Everett said softly. Jack almost smiled.

"About ten years coming," Tony said evenly. "Get your divorce—or not. I really don't give a shit anymore." He looked briefly at the stunned crowd and then walked around the bar and pulled a six-pack from the bottom fridge, the bartender hastily stepping out of his way. He went to the front door and without another word left the house. Regaining himself, Jack went over to the chair where Drew sat quietly as tears ran full course into rivers and began to erode the caked makeup. It gave her a mask-like expression of horror.

"Drew . . . are you alright?"

"Oh damn you. Get away from me . . . all of you. Get *AWAY* from me!" she shrieked. Everett tugged his arm.

"We'd better go, Jack."

"Yeah, I guess so." Moments later they were driving toward Del Monte Avenue, which would connect to The Wharf and around The Bay to Jack's house. They picked up two six-packs of Monterey's finest. Neither spoke until past Cannery Row.

"You sure know how to show a fella a good time. I'd say that for sure," Everett said.

"God, I'm sorry about all this," Jack replied, popping the can tab as he pulled into his driveway. "I don't think I realized how bad these people were until tonight. Christ, we were better behaved years ago when I was on The Hill. I was *friends* with these people?"

"Not all your fault, Jack. You never saw it coming. Hard to convince a fella what something is when he wishes it wasn't. I'm not into hitting the fairer sex, mind you, but even this country gentleman has to conclude that she had it coming. Probably for a long, long time."

"I've never seen him stand up to her. Not like that anyway."

"Well, he sure as hell stood up to her tonight . . . and then some. She'll have to divorce him now just for appearance sake after doing that in front of all those people," Everett said.

"I don't know. Maybe, maybe not. This half plays by different rules."

"The better half," Everett laughed. "Glad I spent all those years working toward it. Real nice crowd." The two stepped into the house and smelled the ocean's saline mist as they closed the door behind them. Many more of Monterey's finest were consumed that night and early into the morning, the intoxicants loosening the nostalgia between genuine friends not bonded by pretense or fortune.

CHAPTER 14

Jack took Everett to brunch at the café where Drew had once met him months before. Both had hangovers, especially Everett, whose general tolerance was not nearly as fortified as Jack's. Jack's system was accustomed to nightly ambushes since his arrival in May. A bottle of Chablis sat on ice at their table next to a plate of strawberries, which was about all Everett's stomach would handle that morning.

"White wine and fruit for breakfast," he said. "The missus would not approve."

"That's how they do it here," Jack replied, swirling his glass—a habit unconsciously picked up over the summer. "Wouldn't want to short you on the Monterey experience. A stop at Bully's and I'll have fulfilled my end as tour guide."

"Why not. I'm on a mini-vacation anyway. Then back to the farm tomorrow. It's been interesting, Jack, but I don't think I could live here."

"Sometimes I wonder myself. I thought coming back would be . . . different," Jack said, as he contemplated the gentle crashes of water in the distance. It was a sunny morning, giving the brighter child of The Bay's Gemini twins.

"You thought the money would *make* it different. Money can't change disposition, Jack. And may the Lord help you if it ever does," Everett said. They finished their breakfast on the second glass of wine. Taking a leisurely roll down to The Row, the two made their way to Bully's. It was Sunday, and the last of the tourists were slow to awake. Like Jack and Everett, they were also recovering from their own previous indulgences as the remnants of the fog rolled over the foothills, cleansing the morning from the misdemeanors of the night before. The lounge was empty when they entered, save two staff members who stood at the bar in bored conversation with one patron who wore a souvenir stating he did indeed witness the famed great white shark and all received was the lousy shirt. Jack walked to him briskly.

"Sarge! I'll be damned!" Jack said. "Thought I'd seen the last of you for good."

Sarge shook his hand. "Nope, just the last time behind the bar counter."

"I know. I heard all about it from our favorite mouth. I'm really sorry for my end of it."

"Nothing to be sorry about, Jack. I probably shouldn't have opened my big trap around their type. But I was due out anyway. I stayed the last few months only from habit for the most part." Jack introduced him to Everett.

"What's your real name, anyway," Jack asked, after buying a round of the lighter lager.

"Kevin. Kevin Pratte," he answered. "Nice of you to finally ask. No one ever asked me the whole year I was here. Your pals kind of pinned 'Sarge' on me the first month. Thought they were being clever. To tell you the truth, I never really liked it much, coming from a bunch of uppity civilians."

"I figured so," Jack replied. "So where are you headed next station?"

"Fort Benning. Officer Candidate School. Put in the paperwork months ago. Now that I've finished the degree, the army, in their infinite wisdom, deems it necessary to put lieutenant bars on my shoulders."

"I'll be damned. Congratulations Sar . . . Kevin. Karma pays in full in the end, I guess."

"Speaking of karma. I heard about the little spat at the Bledsloe domain."

"Spat?" Everett jumped in. "Should have seen it. He knocked the living hell out of her."

"Can't say that bothers me a whole hell of a lot. Like they say, what comes around and all." Jack filled him in on the previous night in specific detail, from their entrance to the party, right up to the implosion of Tony's hand on his wife's face. The ex-bartender just shook his head slowly.

"All that money and some people still can't keep their shit together," Pratte said. Suddenly, Miles burst through the door. He glanced around hurriedly, found Jack and stepped over quickly, barely nodding to the others.

"Pull up a seat, Miles, I'm buying," Jack said. "Miles, you remember from the party my partner in crime, Everett. And although disguised as a civilian, you may recognize Kevin, aka and forever nullified—Sarge."

"Sure, thanks—whatever you're having," Miles said, giving a broad wave to the others at the bar. He took a sip of the beer placed in front of him, and then sat back. "Jack, you heard the news?"

"Nope, after last night we've been in seclusion, just slowly destroying our livers in penance."

"Tony's been arrested."

"So, Drew did call the police?"

"No, no, Jack. When you left after the . . . incident, Drew went up to her room. She never came back down. We all departed shortly after on our own. I'm talking about the feds, Jack. They raided his dad's main office early this morning. Stormed in with guns, badges—the whole works. Confiscated all the files and computers. They got Tony coming back to his house from wherever he went last night. The company wasn't doing as well as Tony let on all this time. I had a feeling. Bad economy affects construction big time. No one was buying drywall much. He cooked the books for the investors, Jack. On a colossal scale. False profit margins. Falsification of expenses for write offs. Clients that didn't exist. Everything. Right under his dad's nose. He's in jail right now downtown."

"Jesus, Miles! And his dad?"

"Never took him. Like I said, apparently had no idea from what I gather, and I'm only getting the sketchy details. But the details are that it's all Tony's doing."

"Where's Drew?"

"Meeting her attorney sometime today. They're quits, Jack."

"What comes around . . . ." Pratte said. He almost broke into a full grin.

"Yeah, sorry about all that, Sarge. It was a bum deal. You know once Drew gets mad . . . "

"Actually, he's not a Sarge anymore," Jack interrupted. "Pretty soon—what do you say, Kevin . . . fifteen weeks and old Sarge here will be a Sir." Pratte winked at him as Miles sat confused with the military rhetoric.

"He's going to be an officer, Miles," Jack continued. "Probably retire as a major, and then go to work for Government Service for six figures a year. Not too bad for an army guy, huh?"

"Good for you, Sarge. I'm glad for you."

"Thanks," Pratte answered, facing forward.

"Listen, guys, I have to go," Miles said, standing up. "My home phone and cell have been ringing off the hook. This is big news, you know. Tony had contracts all over the city. Not the kind of thing we like for publicity."

"I'll bet," Everett said. Miles left the glass of lager and scurried out of the lounge area, the mobile already glued to his ear. At the door, he turned.

"I'll see you around, Jack?"

"Probably not so much, Miles. I think I'm going to lay low for awhile."

"I understand. We're all snobs, I know, but at least we can be civil snobs. Drew can be a real bitch sometimes."

"Drew is a bitch, Miles," Jack replied.

"Yeah, probably. But I hope you come around once in a while. We're ok, right?"

"We're ok, Miles. No hard feelings." Miles nodded as whoever he dialed picked up. He left and walked briskly up the sidewalk, past the window and gave the threesome inside one last wave.

"I'll be goddamned," Jack said softly.

"It's a sad thing to see a man crumble," Everett added. "Especially when he does it to himself."

Jack said his goodbyes to Sarge, aka Kevin, who returned to the barkeep and waitress at the other end of the lounge. He took Everett away from Monterey to the Big Sur area on 17 Mile Drive. They spent the day on the long beaches, exposed by the lifted fog. The next morning Everett left for San Francisco's International Airport in a taxi much to Jack's protest.

"I can give you a ride, Everett."

"And I can afford the transport, Jack," Everett said. "Besides, I have to stop and mull a bit downtown. Shirley will feed me to the hogs if I don't pick up something for her and the kids. I'll spend a few days recovering my aching head and call you. Next time you come up to the farm."

"Deal," Jack replied, shaking his hand. He saw his friend off, the taxi pulled Everett away and down the shoreline toward Highway 1. Then he walked to his cove to clear his own aching head.

CHAPTER 15

October

The afternoon was a dampish cool as fall approached, pushing and shoving the remaining tourists of the season over the green foothills that surrounded The Bay, jettisoning them back to the midlands. Jack sat in the midst of his cove. He watched the cold whitecaps continue their indifference to his presence as they did with the poor and wealthy generations before him who once lulled there.

He had just returned from Everett's farm, where the two had spent soberly days and evenings with the first designs to tweak the MAT. Shirley had introduced Jack to one of her single friends who taught grade school in their rural area. She and Jack's common roots were already deeply planted in the few weeks he spent in the small, nondescript town with Everett's family. Jack wasn't certain on the viability of long distance relationships, only that gain did indeed come from venture.

Cannery Row had been uncommon ground the last month as Jack's visits to Tony consisted of what he saw on the local news, which recently announced that his father had suffered a fatal heart attack during the turmoil. His father's death finally gave Tony full rights to the corporation, which was now under federal assault. Sarge had left Monterey weeks ago, on his way to better company.

Jack returned to his habit of a few beers a week and ran in the mornings consistently. He looked and felt rejuvenated as the previous four month veil lifted from his eyes. He decided one Saturday to stop by Bully's to satisfy his curiosity of local gossip, now that the tourists were well out of earshot.

As he entered the lounge, he unsurprisingly saw Drew and Miles sitting in the corner. A formal wave from the table was given with no indication that the event should be enhanced by his company, which slightly hurt but mostly relieved him.

He sat at the bar and ordered a lager. A moment later, Drew came over with a new mask, which couldn't conceal the sleepless nights and drawn face that attempted to stretch into a smile.

"Jack," she said cheerily. "How have you been?"

"How have *you* been, Drew?"

"Simply marvelous, of course. You have heard, I assume, that Tony and I are getting a divorce. He won't contest it obviously. Nice and tidy. Should be finalized at the end of the month."

"I'm sorry, Drew," he said automatically.

"Now, my dear Jack, don't be all humdrum. Perhaps we started all wrong—you and I. We should get together sometime and talk, of course. Become friends again. I always liked you, Jack—surely you know that?"

"I don't think so, Drew."

"Oh," she said with mock amusement. "I see then. Well, this is my new number anyway if you change your mind—and I *do* hope you change it, Jack." He took the number, saying nothing, folded it and stuck it into his front pocket, knowing he would never unfold it. Drew waited an appropriate moment until the silence began to make her uncomfortable as Jack stared straight ahead.

"Ok then, I'll see you around, I suppose, Jack," she said briskly as he lifted two fingers in a semi-wave. She returned to Miles. They talked quietly, and then left their drinks moments later. An hour afterward he felt a tap on his shoulder. To his surprise, it was Tony, who looked worn and haggard. Like a man who had a few continents on his shoulders.

"Sorry about your dad, Tony," he said, shaking his hand, which had lost the once powerful grip he had experienced in May.

"Oh, thanks, Pop was . . . a good man. Better than his son at running things as you have heard," he said, trying to lighten the predicament for Jack's benefit. "I'm sure you've also gotten wind of the trial?"

"What's going to happen, Tony?"

"I'm going to spend two or three years in federal prison. My lawyer already told me that when I plea bargain. They have to hang the nobleman once in awhile. It's not the penitentiary, but it's not Monterey either."

"Christ, Tony."

"I guess I had my due coming, old boy. You know, I'm not a bad man, Jack.

I just got caught up in it. I never sided with Drew on anything between you and her."

"I kind of figured that after you hit her," Jack said.

"It's true. Not in my character . . . what little remains of it. I drank too much that night. But hell, what night don't I drink too much? Started about three years after being married to . . . her. I guess temperance is coming since I don't think there is a Bully's in the joint. Do they really call it the joint?"

"I don't know, Tony."

"Pop's—or should I say *my* company is on the market. After the huge fines and money to the stockholders I'll have to pay and divorce settlement, I'll still have a few hundred thousand left, my financial guru says."

"Good." They sat quietly for a few minutes.

"You must think I'm a louse," Tony said.

"No, I think we're just very different. You didn't notice in the beginning because of the money. But we are different—me and all of you."

"Possibly. Maybe I just had it too easy. Pop and his dad built everything, you know. All I got was the end product. Didn't have to get my hands dirty. Maybe I took it for granted. But I won't be taking anything for granted after the trial, old boy. You can bet on that. Have to start over—on my own. Nothing for granted this time."

"Probably not."

"Going to leave Monterey when I get out. Hell, I won't be able to afford to live here. Never realized how expensive it was until the rug got yanked. I'll get some regular exec job, I hope. I still have Yale on my resume."

"I hope so, Tony."

"Anyway, I won't be around much—not very comfortable being stared at all the time. Can't even hide in the midst of the tourists now. You take care of yourself, Jack. Send me some cigarettes when I'm in?"

"You bet," Jack said. Tony left in good humor but with slumped shoulders of a fighter, who raises his hands after the final bell, fully knowing he was beaten badly. Jack watched him disappear down the sidewalk, feeling only pity for the man.

"No one's going to hire him with a record, Yale or not," said a new barmaid who had been eavesdropping the last few minutes of the conversation. "Even I know that from community business 101."

"I know," Jack replied sadly. He left the pub shortly after his second beer, keeping the prior habit and slowly walked home along the shoreline that rose from Cannery Row. He listened faintly to the crashing waves as the sun descended over The Bay, which gave the shimmering blue the first hints of winter gray.

AUTHOR'S NOTE

In early 1991, I lived in a small, grubby, one-room efficiency in Cincinnati, Ohio, and worked for exactly 8.64 an hour as a Correctional Officer for the Hamilton County Justice Department while I tried to figure a means to improve myself via college, which was almost insurmountable without assistance of some sort. I was twenty-two and saw my general situation unchanged at thirty-two unless I took drastic action. So, like many young men without means or idea on achieving means, I entered active duty service via the United States Army, a common orphanage for the poor and wayward.

Ironically, I was stationed in one of the most affluent cities in the nation—Monterey, California. I was to study Polish on "The Hill" at the Defense Language Institute for a year before being placed at a permanent duty station. California was a childhood dream and at the time I felt myself fortunate to fulfill that dream through the vast generosity of the military. I left for Monterey in February of 1991 with one duffel bag—the rest of my meager possessions kept in a storage locker in Cincinnati.

It would be safe to say that soldiers were not welcomed with open arms in the "native" community. I had believed that it was partly due to the general roughness of the defenders of our nation but it was much more to an inherent snobbery of a community that had neither volunteered nor been forced by desperation to wear the uniform. To say that we were treated unkindly would be a vast understatement. The locals regarded us quite as untouchables. It was common to be ignored in their shops and stores if one's hair was of significant cut. Sometimes even for the officers. A slightly devastating blow when you're twenty-two years old and aren't incredibly satisfied with your position as a Private First Class, only to have the entire community deem you correct in your judgment. Like young Jack Strickland, there was an English Pub of quaint style that I spent a Friday or Saturday night in, drinking Harp beer while mystified that the glaring natives did not appreciate us coming down "The Hill" into what they considered their quarters.

Twelve years later after the trials and tribulations of becoming an accepted member of the medical community and independent contractor, I returned to the same bay, which was located two hours drive from my contract positions in Central Valley, California. I was in much higher standing than when I departed from it. The same sweetly rotten fragrance of the surf and kelp brought back the vivid memory of riding down Del Monte Avenue in a cab that first sign in day at DLI in 1991. I now had the slightly graying goatee and lightly lined face, which signified that I was no longer part of the young untouchables who still served there.

While contracting in Central Valley, I visited my old stomping grounds probably fifteen to twenty times in the next five years—walking the shoreline path past Jack's cove (it's located at Ocean View Blvd. and Fifth, then turn left for about thirty yards) to Lover's Point and back to The Row and The Wharf. Now quite able to afford the expensive dinners and drinks without the self consciousness of hostile looks, I was able to observe the natives and the tourists together more acutely. I would listen to their conversations while glued to the bar at Bullwackers—the real life version of Bully's where the natives were known to congregate on Cannery Row. The first few times revisiting, I deemed that possibly I misunderstood these people, being a young twenty-two-year-old full of attitude who was thrust into their midst so long ago.

I found that I did not. Of course, Monterey is not exclusive in demeanor of the upper society but certainly symbolizes them in general terms. How people born into wealth are molded in beliefs, attitude and opinion.

And that general opinion was that somehow being born into privilege elevates one into a noble class that is superior to everyone else. They grow up in neighborhoods where the women can run along the shoreline at night without threat of harm, go to the upper echelon universities without a worry of finance, and then are reintegrated back into their own by their own. They believe to have an understanding of the factory worker when they have never worked the line themselves. They have answers for policy for the military when they never wore the uniform. They have dozens of acquaintances but no real friends, frequenting downtown with forced trivial speech, false sincerity, loveless marriages and a general lack of understanding or empathy for the human condition, which outside of their velvet ropes isn't nearly as nice as they perceive it to be.

Drew and Beverly, portrayed as a typical native girl, who one can recognize today by the sharply dressed attire, donned in expensive sunglasses and finely salon tuned hair, who will switch to skintight shorts and a halter top while interrupting her life of leisure for the daily run on the beach. She is actually a vivid memory of a privileged girl who went slumming and ended up with the likes of me, living in sin for nine months in Indianapolis. But the privileged product of wealth is the same whether in Indianapolis, Monterey, New York or Berlin. Like Jack, I came dangerously close to marrying her, which would have resulted in an empty bank account and depleted soul, much like Tony, his psyche slowly whittled down years later. Miles was created from a conversation I had with two very civil young city workers at a bar in Monterey, who although pleasant, had absolutely no clue of the makings of the real world. Tony was developed from a real life character who I met in Bullwackers and shared Rum Runners with. He was an ex-athlete and very well off financially but not spiritually, realizing too late that the cheers from the stands had died long ago.

What is startling about Tony, Drew, Miles and Beverly is not their character persona but that they are based on real life experiences. These people do exist in our midst, granted their extravagant lives by the effort of predecessors. They are programmed from birth with formulated belief systems in the Ivy vacuums of ultra-high education. Like Jack Strickland, I found my return of nostalgia only further marked my disillusionment and disdain for a class that is quite unoriginal, existing in an intellectual void, filled with borrowed abstract thoughts and purchased lives.

During the summer of 2009 as I had determined to leave the crumbling remnants of California for good, I disappeared into the wilderness via backpack into the Sierras and Trinity Alps to contemplate the nature of man. Just prior to my exit into the mountains, I stayed at the Green Gables Inn in Monterey—a ritzy bed and breakfast, directly across from Jack's shoreline path. I am in no way an adoring fan of extravagance but felt this farewell trip was sweet revenge for one who entered Monterey as a lower enlisted soldier and was to exit as a successful medical contractor. I had already finished the first edit of my much longer novel. Also, I had been sober for four months and with cleared eyes could keenly observe the "natives" again in their natural setting, without the coursing of Jack's Rummers or gin and tonics or endless local lagers in my system, which had been prior, my usual habit there. And what I observed for the final time, now eighteen years later, became the making of *The Monterians,* which originally started out as a short story. A rant, if you will, to get out of my system the remaining anger that still lingered toward the locals there almost two decades later. The rant, however, built steam and blew into a novel written on my notebook in the wilderness. First draft was completed in Nevada's Ruby Mountains where I was isolated, far away from the elitist society I detested. Only now, upon final completion, do I feel avenged, not only for myself but for all who have been made to feel inferior by those existing in unearned and undeserved prestige.

C.H.

August, 2011

LIKE THE BOOK? HELP SELF-PUBLISHED AUTHORS BY LEAVING A REVIEW ON AMAZON. THANKS AND SAFE JOURNEY TO YOU IN YOUR LIFE.